PENGUIN BOOKS
STAINED GLASS ELEGIES

Shusaku Endo was born in Tokyo in 1923. After his parents divorced, he and his mother converted to Roman Catholicism. He graduated in French literature from Keio University, then studied for several years in Lyons on a scholarship from the French government. The leading Japanese writer of today, Shusaku Endo has won many major literary awards: the Akutagawa Prize, the Mainichi Cultural Prize, the Shincho Prize, the Tanizaki Prize and the Noma Prize. In 1981 he was elected to the Nihon geijutsuin, the Japanese Arts Academy. He contributes to newspapers and magazines and has his own television show. He lives in Tokyo and pays regular visits to the West.

His work has received widespread acclaim. His other books include *Silence*, which Graham Greene called 'one of the finest novels of our time'; *The Sea of Poison*; *Volcano*; *When I Whistle*, of which A. N. Wilson said, 'Endo is always a moralist. But *When I Whistle* shows him to be a great artist as well'; *The Samurai*; *Scandal*, which was called 'a remarkable work' by the *Listener* and described in the London *Evening Standard* as 'a subtle, eerie and fascinating book by a writer of rare perception and disquieting honesty'; *Wonderful Fool* and *Foreign Studies*.

D1393103

SHUSAKU ENDO

STAINED GLASS ELEGIES

TRANSLATED BY
VAN C. GESSEL

PENGUIN BOOKS

PENGUIN BOOKS

Published by the Penguin Group
27 Wrights Lane, London w8 5TZ, England
Viking Penguin Inc., 40 West 23rd Street, New York, New York 10010, USA
Penguin Books Australia Ltd, Ringwood, Victoria, Australia
Penguin Books Canada Ltd, 2801 John Street, Markham, Ontario, Canada L3R 1B4
Penguin Books (NZ) Ltd, 182–190 Wairau Road, Auckland 10, New Zealand

Penguin Books Ltd, Registered Offices: Harmondsworth, Middlesex, England

This selection first published by Peter Owen 1984
Published in Penguin Books 1986
3 5 7 9 10 8 6 4 2

Made and printed in Great Britain by
Richard Clay Ltd, Bungay, Suffolk
Typeset in Ehrhardt

Contents

Translator's Introduction

Over the last ten years the novels of Shūsaku Endō have received widespread attention in the West, and his name can confidently be added to that short list of Japanese authors familiar to and admired by readers in Europe and the United States. A fair estimation of his literary importance can be made on the basis of the six novels, one play, and the contemplative biography of Jesus that have appeared in English translation. Many of his important serious works are now available for each individual reader and critic to judge.

What is not so easy to convey to his foreign admirers, however, is the vast range of Shūsaku Endō's literary talents. The image of Endō which has been created in the West is certainly accurate, but only partially so. For he is widely known in Japan not only as a novelist, but also as the author of finely-crafted short stories, of miscellaneous, often humorous essays, and of varied works in other genres that have yet to make the transition into English.

This is to some extent unfortunate, for those who can read him in Japanese recognize many facets to Mr Endō's talents, and have perhaps a more rounded view of the overall significance of his work. The eleven short stories translated here, written over the two decades between 1959 and 1977, will, I hope, make a few more pieces of the puzzle available to his expanding Western audience. The stories were selected (in consultation with Mr Endō) with the aim of demonstrating the range of the author's talents in the short story form. They are, with two exceptions ('Despicable Bastard' and 'Incredible Voyage'), taken from two short story collections published in Japan. The first, *Aika* ('Elegies'), appeared in 1965; it contained eleven stories, many of them dealing with Shūsaku Endō's lengthy hospitalization for massive lung surgery. The second anthology, *Jūichi no iro garasu* ('Eleven Stained-Glass Segments'), was published in 1979. In both content and title, *Stained Glass Elegies* is a composite of these two works.

The first story, 'A Forty-Year-Old Man', is in Japan one of the most admired and most frequently anthologized of Endō's stories. It was published in a literary journal in 1964, shortly after his release from hospital. It introduces a significant literary symbol – the myna bird, a sorrowful, priestly figure that observes the hero's actions with pity, not condemnation – which would later be fleshed out as Endō's image of a forgiving Christ. The underlying philosophy of the story, that 'the actions of a human being are never self-contained', is central to Endō's view of human interrelationships and of the need for personal responsibility.

'Despicable Bastard' of 1959 is the earliest story in this collection; it appeared the same year as his novel *Wonderful Fool*. Like many of his other stories, 'Despicable Bastard' is derived from Endō's own background; as a college student during the war, he lived in a Christian dormitory in Tokyo, and the experiences at the Gotemba leper hospital are essentially his own. The story conveys not only the fear of physical suffering common to his longer works, but also, in its concluding scene, provides a perfect metaphor for Japan's war generation, to which Endō belongs. Caught in the middle during the war – unable to protest, unwilling to fight – Endō's generation continues to carry the scars of the survivor. Endō was actually one of the more fortunate members of his generation; he could at least rely upon his religious faith, and upon the compassionate example of those, like the lepers in this story, who turned their own weaknesses into virtues.

'My Belongings' was originally published in 1963. Endō had been deeply affected by the conversion to Catholicism of his close friend, the novelist Miura Shumon (Mita in the story), and the baptism of another literary colleague, Shimao Toshio (called Nagao here). Those two events caused Endō to reflect on his own unwitting acceptance of Christianity and the other examples of seemingly haphazard fate that had shaped his life. His belief in the need for an individual to embrace those moments of chance and cling to them is portrayed vividly in this short work.

Endō's fascination with Father Maximilian Kolbe long antedates that priest's recent canonization. 'Fuda-no-Tsuji' is one of several works, including the novel *Shikai no hotori* ('By the Shores of the Dead Sea') and the recent story '*Warushawa no Nipponjin*' ('Japanese in Warsaw'), that deal with Father Kolbe's sojourn in Japan. The events in these works are imagined – except for Kolbe's eventual martyrdom – but they convey a sense of Endō's continued interest in the weakling who can sacrifice himself, not out of courage or for the sake of any dogmatic principle, but solely as the result of a boundless love for others.

'The Day Before', written in 1963, is a story told with gentle humour, providing an affecting portrait of a rather seedy character. In it, Endō pursues another of the images that has inflamed his literary imagination over the years – the *fumie*. Here, however, it is a curiously modern, decidedly human incarnation of the holy image which lies at the core of the story.

In 1968 Endō published one of the most zestful and delightful of his humorous stories, 'Incredible Voyage'. Superficially it is a parody of the 1966 American film *Fantastic Voyage*. The lengths to which Endō goes in his pastiche may be surprising; even more remarkable, however, is the fact that this story has a good deal in common with his serious works. The naïve young doctor, Bontarō (his name means 'mediocre' in Japanese), is drawn to the inner beauty of the woman he loves and realizes that it is her character rather than her physical appearance that is most appealing. This is certainly little different from Endō's long-standing interest in the essence rather than the superficialities of Christianity and the character of its founder. And of course the hospital setting in this story provides a marvellous contrast to the sombre, forbidding hospital wards that Endō often describes.

'Unzen', published in 1965, is essentially a preliminary sketch for the character of Kichijirō, who would appear as a major figure in the novel published the following year, *Silence*. This is one of Endō's many attempts to place himself beside the main characters in his historical narratives and examine the similarities between them. His is a unique approach to the familiar tradition of autobiographical fiction in modern Japan.

'Mothers' (1969) is easily the most intensely personal and the most important short story that Endō has produced. Written in the wake of *Silence* and underscored by Endō's growing realization that his unique image of Christ was partly based on his own feelings toward his mother, this superbly constructed tale emphasizes the forgiving, maternal side of Christ as viewed by the *kakure*, a group of underground Christians in Kyushu.

'Retreating Figures' (1976) is typical of Endō's recent stories: the tone is more mellow, the Christian concerns more subtly absorbed into the fabric of his fiction. This calm, philosophical mode is the distinguishing feature of much of Endō's work over the past few years, culminating in *The Samurai* of 1980.

'The War Generation', published in 1977, is another story in which the Second World War is a major motif. Although he never served in the

Japanese military, Endō has clearly been influenced by his experiences during those years, and his views of human frailty, egotism and complicity can all be traced back to common roots in the war. The main character in 'The War Generation' shares many attitudes with Ozu, the protagonist of *When I Whistle*. Endō draws an elaborate series of contrasts between wartime and the present day in this story, but he scrupulously avoids painting either period in a romantic light. His concern is with the realities that confront the war generation – the group with perhaps the greatest sense of personal and national loss in the history of Japanese civilization.

The collection ends on a recessional note with 'Old Friends' of 1977. Here again Endō exposes shadows of the war, but his focus is less on recalled pain than on the bonds of friendship that have allowed those of his generation to endure the isolation of the postwar era. The ending of the story demonstrates a fundamental optimism that some of Endō's Western readers have overlooked. I hope this collection of stories will illuminate the subtle but definite affirmation of hope that has emerged from Endō's personal and literary struggles over the years. While 'A Forty-Year-Old Man' concludes on a note of muted despair, with the protagonist doubting to himself that 'everything will be all right now', in 'Old Friends' the pain of human betrayal is somewhat assuaged, and there are indications that the benevolence of the individual can overcome all forms of cruelty: 'I only feel pain in the winter when it is cold. When spring comes, I am fine again. That is the way it always is.'

Van C. Gessel
University of California, Berkeley
January 1984

A FORTY-YEAR-OLD MAN

People sometimes wonder *when* they will die, Suguro realized. But they never give much thought to *where* they will breathe their last.

No matter who dies in a hospital, the staff handle death as if they were mailing a package at the post office.

One evening the man in the next room, who suffered from intestinal cancer, died. For a time Suguro could hear the weeping voices of the man's family. Eventually some nurses went into the room, loaded the corpse onto a cart, and wheeled it down to the morgue. The following morning the cleaning woman was humming a tune as she sterilized the vacated room. Later that same afternoon, another patient would be admitted. No one would tell him that a man had died in his room the previous evening, and the new patient would of course have no way of obtaining that information.

The sky is cloudless. Dinner is brought around to the hospital rooms as usual, as though nothing at all has happened. On the streets below, beyond the windows of the hospital, cars and buses race by. Everyone is concealing something.

Two weeks before the day scheduled for his third operation, Suguro had his wife buy a myna bird. That particular kind of bird was considerably more expensive than a finch or a canary, and when he made the suggestion, a faint look of distress flashed across her face. But she nodded 'All right,' and forced a smile. Her cheeks had become thinner over the long months of caring for her husband.

In the course of his illness, Suguro had seen this smile many times. On the day the doctor had held the still-damp X-rays up to the light and declared, 'With lesions like this, we're going to have to operate,' his wife had produced that unwavering smile in an attempt to salve his troubled mind. He had in fact been left speechless for some time when the doctors announced that they would be removing six of his ribs. In the middle of the night after that painful operation, when he had awakened still drowsy from the anaesthetic, the first thing he had seen was this smile on his wife's face. Even when the second operation ended in failure and Suguro felt completely drained of life, that smile never fled from her face.

His three years in the hospital had whittled down their bank account to virtually nothing. Undoubtedly it was inconsiderate of him to ask her to use part of their dwindling funds to buy an expensive myna bird. But right now Suguro had a reason for wanting the bird.

His wife seemed to regard the request as merely the whim of an ailing man, for she nodded and said, 'I'll get one at the department store tomorrow.'

At dusk the next day, she came into the room carrying a large package in either arm. Their son followed along behind. It was a depressingly overcast December day. One of the packages contained his freshly-laundered pyjamas and underwear. He could hear the faint rustling of a bird inside the other package, which was wrapped in a cloth with an arabesque pattern.

'Was it expensive?'

'Don't worry about it. They knocked something off the price for me.'

Their five-year-old son crouched excitedly in front of the cage and peered inside.

Vivid yellow stripes trimmed the neck of the stark-black myna bird. It sat frozen on its perch, its chest feathers quivering – perhaps the train journey had been unsettling.

'Now you won't be all alone when we go home.'

Nights in the hospital were dark and long. Relatives were not allowed to stay in the rooms after 6 p.m. He always ate dinner alone, then stretched out alone on his bed, with nothing to do but stare at the ceiling.

'Feeding it is quite a business. The man told me you have to dissolve the feed in water and then shape it into a ball about the size of your thumb.'

'Won't it choke on something that big?'

'No. He said it helps them learn to imitate all kinds of voices.' She went into the kitchen provided for patients' use. Preparing part of his diet was one of her responsibilities.

The boy poked at the bird with his finger, and it crouched panic-stricken in one corner of the cage. 'Daddy, they said this bird can talk. Will you teach him to say some things before I come next time?'

Suguro smiled and nodded to his son, who had been born in the maternity ward of this hospital nearly six years before. 'Sure. What should I teach him? Would you like me to get him to say your name?'

Evening haze began to coil around the hospital room. Outside the window dim lights flickered in each of the wings of the hospital. A squeaky food wagon passed down the corridor.

Suguro's wife returned with a plate of food. 'The house is empty tonight, so we ought to be heading back.' She wrapped the plate in cellophane and set it on a chair. 'You've got to eat all of this whether you're hungry or not. You must build up your strength before the operation.'

At his mother's prodding, the boy said, 'Goodbye, Daddy. Take care of yourself.' At the door his wife turned back once more and said, 'Keep fighting.'

And that smile lit up her face again.

His room was suddenly quiet. With a flutter the myna bird darted about its cage. Sitting on his bed, Suguro peered into the mournful eyes of the bird. He recognized that it had been capricious of him, but he had several reasons for imploring his wife to buy this expensive bird.

Ever since the failure of his second operation, followed by the decision that one entire lung would have to be removed, the necessity of seeing people had pained Suguro. The doctors always spoke confidently when they talked to him about the approaching surgery, but he could tell from their expressions and from the way they avoided his eyes that the chances of success were slim. His problems were complicated by the fact that after his second abortive operation, the pleurae had adhered tightly to the walls of his chest. The greatest danger posed by the imminent surgery was the massive haemorrhaging that would occur when those adhesions were stripped away. He had already heard stories of several patients in the same predicament who had died on the operating table. He no longer had the strength to greet visitors and joke with them, feigning high spirits. A myna bird seemed the ideal companion.

As the age of forty crept up on him, Suguro began to derive pleasure from studying the eyes of dogs and birds. Viewed from one angle, those eyes seemed cold and inhuman; yet from another perspective they appeared to brim with sorrow. He had once raised a pair of finches, but one of them had died. He had held the tiny bird in the palm of his hand before it expired. Once or twice it struggled to open its eyes, as though in final desperate defiance of the white membrane of death that was gradually stealing across its pupils.

He came to be aware of eyes filled with a similar sorrow observing his own life. Suguro felt particularly that those eyes had been fixed on him since the events of a day many years past. The eyes were riveted on him, as if they were trying to tell him something.

2

A bronchoscope test was one of the required pre-operative examinations. A metal tube with a mirror attached was plunged directly down the patient's throat and into the bronchi to examine them. Because of the miserable position they had to assume for the test – stretched out on the examination table with the metal rod thrust down their throats – the patients called this test 'The Barbecue'. It was all the nurses could do to hold down their victims as they writhed in pain and coughed up blood and spittle from their throats.

When the test was completed and Suguro limped back to his room, wiping the blood from his battered gums, his wife and son were waiting for him.

'Your face is as white as a sheet.'

'I had a test. The barbecued chicken thing.'

By now Suguro was numb to physical pain, and it no longer frightened him.

'Daddy, how's the myna bird?'

'He hasn't learned to say anything yet.'

Suguro sat on the edge of the bed and tried to calm his irregular breathing.

'Just before we left, Yasuko called from Ōmori. She said she and her husband were coming over today to see you.' His wife had her back to him, tying on an apron as she spoke, so he could not read the expression on her face.

'With her husband?'

'Uh-huh.'

Yasuko was his wife's cousin. Four years ago she had married an official of the Economic Planning Agency. One look at the man's sturdy neck and broad shoulders and Suguro was impressed that he had seen the model of the aggressive businessman.

Suguro lapsed into silence. His wife seemed to feel some constraint and ventured, 'Yasuko could . . . If you're worn out from the tests, I can call and tell her not to come.'

'No, it's all right. If they're going to the trouble of coming . . .'

He lay down on the bed. Pillowing his head on his arms, he stared up at the ceiling, which was stained with rain leaks. The borders of the stains had yellowed. It had been raining on *that* night, too. In a confessional smaller and darker than this hospital room, he had knelt down, separated by a metal grille from an old foreign priest who reeked of wine.

'*Misereatur tui Omnipotens Deus . . .*'

The old priest lifted one hand and intoned the Latin prayer, then turned his head to the side and waited quietly for Suguro to speak.

'I . . .' Suguro began, then paused. For a long while he had debated whether to come to this chamber and confess what he had done. Finally he had summoned the courage and come here, hoping to tear off the gauze and diseased flesh that clung to his wound.

'I . . .' *I . . . When I was a child, I was baptized because my parents wanted me to be, not because I wanted to. As a result, I went to church for many years as a formality, because it had become a habit. But after that particular day, I knew that I could never cast off the ill-fitting clothes my parents had dressed me in.* Over the years those clothes themselves had adhered to him, and he knew that if he discarded them, he would be left with no protection for his body or his soul.

'Hurry,' the priest urged him quietly, the smells of wine and of his own foul breath spewing together from his mouth. 'The next person is waiting.'

'I haven't been to Mass for a long time. My daily actions have been lacking in charity . . .' One after another Suguro let the inconsequential sins spill forth. 'I have not been an exemplary husband or father in my home.'

These words are absurd! I'm here on my knees muttering absolutely ridiculous phrases! Through his mind flashed the faces of friends who would mock him if they could see him now. His words were more than ridiculous – they were filled with a vile hypocrisy that had become a part of him.

This was not what he had come to say. The matter which Suguro felt compelled to confess to the one who stood beyond the reeking old priest had nothing to do with these insignificant, petty transgressions.

'Is that all?'

Suguro sensed that he was about to perform an act of even baser dishonesty.

'Yes. That's all.'

'Recite the Hail Mary three times. Do you understand? He died for the sins of us all . . .' When he had delivered this simple admonition and prescribed the simple penance in an almost mechanical tone, the priest again lifted his hand and chanted a Latin prayer. 'Now . . . go in peace.'

Suguro got up and walked to the door of the tiny chamber. *How can they claim that a person's sins are forgiven through such a perfunctory ceremony?* He could still hear the priest saying, 'He died for the sins of us all . . .' His knees throbbed slightly from kneeling on the floor. Behind him he sensed those sorrowful eyes, staring at him with a pain greater than he had seen in the eyes of the finch that had died in the palm of his hand. . . .

'Good morning. Good morning. Good morning!'

'You'll just confuse the poor bird if you talk that fast.' Suguro got out of bed, put on his slippers, and went out onto the veranda. He crouched next to his son in front of the birdcage. The bird had cocked its head and was listening quizzically to the boy's voice.

'Come on! "Good morning." Say "Good morning!"'

The metal birdcage reminded Suguro of the confessional. A gridwork partition just like this had separated him from the foreign priest. In the end he had not confessed what he had done. He had been unable to speak the words.

'Say it! Why won't you say it, birdie?'

'It can't say it.'

His wife looked at him, surprised by his remark. Suguro stared at the floor. There was a knock at the door, and the white face of a woman peered in. It was Yasuko.

3

'I kept thinking we ought to come see you. I'm really sorry. Even my husband says I'm terrible.'

Yasuko was wearing a white Ōshima kimono with a finely-patterned jacket. She sat down next to her husband and balanced her handbag on her lap.

'These probably aren't any good, but try them anyway,' she said, handing Suguro's wife some cookies from Izumiya. Like Nagasakiya sponge cake, this was a confection which visitors almost invariably felt obliged to bring to a patient in hospital.

And like the cookies, the expression on the face of Yasuko's husband made it obvious that he had come solely out of a sense of obligation towards his relatives. *If I die*, Suguro thought absently, *he'll feel obliged to put on a black arm-band and come to the funeral. But the moment he gets home, he'll have Yasuko sprinkle salt on him to exorcize the pollution of death.*

'Your colour looks very good,' Yasuko was saying. 'I'm sure everything will be all right this time. Why, what could go wrong? All you have to do is convince yourself that bad luck is behind you now.' Then Yasuko turned to her husband to solicit his concurrence. 'Isn't that right?'

'Umm-hmm.'

'My husband's really the one in danger – he's never had a day's illness in his life. He's out partying late every night with business meetings and this and that. They say it's better to be sick once than never at all, so I'll bet your husband will outlive us all. You've got to be careful too, dear.'

'Ummm-hmmm.' Yasuko's husband muttered his assent as he pulled a pack of cigarettes out of his pocket. Then he glanced at Suguro and hurriedly stuffed them back.

'Go ahead and smoke. It doesn't bother me.'

'No.' He shook his head in perplexity.

Yasuko and Suguro's wife began talking amongst themselves. Their conversation apparently dealt with an old friend whom neither Suguro nor Yasuko's husband had heard of. As the topic of conversation shifted to who had married whom, and then to a recital which a certain dance teacher was giving, the two men, excluded from the discussion, could only look at one another in awkward silence.

'That's a lovely obi, Yasuko.'

'Don't be silly. It was cheap.'

Yasuko was wearing a crimson obi with her white Ōshima kimono.

'That crimson suits you very well. Where did you have it made?'

'The Mitsudaya. In Yotsuya . . .'

This was unusual cynicism for his wife. Suguro knew that she thought it was vulgar to wear obis like this one, and he was left to wonder what had prompted this caustic remark to Yasuko. Maybe it was because she didn't have that sort of obi herself. The kimonos and obis she had brought with her when they were married had disappeared one after another. It had dawned on Suguro that without saying anything she had been selling them over the last three years while he had been in the hospital. But he realized now that simple covetousness had not been the only motivation for her remark, and he was startled.

The crimson of Yasuko's obi reminded him of the colour of blood. Blood had spattered the smock of the doctor at the little maternity clinic where he had taken Yasuko. It must have been Yasuko's blood. And, to be more precise, partly his blood, too. The blood of something that had come about between him and Yasuko.

When it had happened several years before, Suguro's wife had been in a bed in the maternity ward of this same hospital. She had not been admitted for delivery. There was considerable danger that the birth would be premature, so she had been put into the hospital for nearly two weeks. If the child were born prematurely, it would weigh less then 700 grams and would have to be cared for in an incubator, so the doctor had given his wife regular injections of special hormones.

Yasuko was still not married then, so she often came to visit Suguro's wife in the hospital. Bringing Bavarian cremes instead of Izumiya cookies. She would toss out the faded flowers in her cousin's room and replace them with roses. The studio where she studied dancing was in nearby Samon-cho, so it was no trouble for her to stop by the hospital on her way home.

Often when the bell rang to signal the end of visiting hours, Suguro would turn up the collar of his overcoat and accompany Yasuko outside. He would turn back to stare at the wing of the maternity ward. With the lights shining in each tiny window, the ward looked like a ship docking at night.

'You're going to have to go back home by yourself and eat alone, aren't you . . . ? That's miserable. You don't have a maid, do you?' Yasuko frequently commented, nestling down into her shawl.

'What am I supposed to do? I can buy a can of something and take it home.'

'If that's what you're going to do . . . I . . . Would you like me to cook dinner for you? How about it?'

Looking back on it now, Suguro was no longer sure whether he had seduced Yasuko or she had tempted him. It made no difference. A relationship – whether love, or a union born of loneliness, or one without any special justification – had swiftly developed between them. When Suguro tugged at her arm, she had spilled over onto him, her eyes narrowed to slits, as if she had been waiting for this. They tumbled together onto the bed which had belonged to Suguro's wife before their marriage. When it was over, Yasuko had sat in front of his wife's mirror stand and, lifting her white arms to her head, had straightened her tousled hair.

The day before his wife was readmitted to the hospital for the actual delivery, Yasuko had fearfully announced to Suguro, 'I think I'm pregnant. What are we going to do?'

His face twisted disgustingly, but he said nothing.

'Oh. You're afraid, aren't you? Yes, of course you are. Because you can't tell me to go ahead and have the child.'

'That not it . . .'

'Coward!' She began to cry.

After his wife was admitted to the hospital, Suguro returned to his deserted house and sat down alone in the small bedroom. The declining sun shone through the window and onto the two beds. One was his wife's bed, where he and Yasuko had come together in an embrace. Suddenly Suguro noticed something small and black glinting like a needle at the edge of the straw mat. It was a woman's hair-pin. He had no way of knowing whether it belonged to his wife, or whether Yasuko had left it behind that day. Suguro held the small black object in the palm of his hand, staring at it for a long while.

On the advice of a friend from his middle-school days, he took Yasuko to a tiny maternity clinic in Setagaya. Unaccustomed to such matters, Suguro did not even know whether he should ask for a 'termination of pregnancy' or an 'abortion'.

'Is this your wife?' When the nurse behind the glass reception window asked the question, Suguro's face stiffened and he could not answer. Beside him, Yasuko responded clearly, 'Yes, I am.'

When she and the nurse had gone inside, he sat down in the small, chilly waiting-room. He thought about the look on Yasuko's face as she had answered, 'Yes, I am.' There had been no trace of vacillation in her expression.

A cockroach darted along the wall of the waiting-room. There was a stain like a handprint on the wall. As he flipped through the pages of the out-of-date, coverless magazine he held on his lap, Suguro's mind naturally was elsewhere. As a baptized Catholic, he was well aware that abortion was prohibited. But he was intimidated by the possibility that his wife and family might find out what he was doing now, and learn of his relationship with Yasuko. He wanted to close his eyes to everything in order to preserve the happiness of his home. Eventually the old doctor opened the door and came out. The bloodstain that raced diagonally across his smock must have come from Yasuko. Instinctively, Suguro looked away. . . .

'We've just come back from Izu,' Yasuko was saying. 'No, not to the hot springs. I went along to carry his golf-clubs. Have you noticed I've started putting on weight? Well, he encouraged me to take up golf, since absolutely everybody is playing golf these days. But I hate doing what everyone else is doing. . . .'

Suguro's wife listened to her cousin's words with that same smile on her face. According to her husband, Yasuko had been trying since childhood to best her cousin in everything. The two girls had studied classical dance together; at a recital, Suguro's wife had danced the *Tamaya*, and Yasuko had wept because she had to dance the less showy *Sagimusume*. It therefore seemed likely that she had brought up the subject of golf now in a conscious attempt to compare her own active husband with the sickly man her cousin had married. The golf enthusiast continued to sit wordlessly across from Suguro, apparently anxious to conclude the tedious visit.

'Is this your wife?' 'Yes, I am.' On the day of Yasuko's wedding, Suguro was able to see that unruffled expression on her face once again.

The new bride and groom stood at the entrance to the hotel reception room, flanked by the go-betweens and nodding repeatedly to the guests who came to offer their congratulations. Suguro and his wife passed along the line and stood before the newlyweds. Yasuko was wearing a wedding dress of pure white. When her eyes met Suguro's, she narrowed them into slits like a Buddhist statue and peered into his face. Then she gently bowed her head.

'Con . . . gratulations,' Suguro breathed in a nearly inaudible voice. The stains on the clinic wall and the splotch of her blood on the doctor's coat darted across his mind like shadow pictures. The bridegroom stood stiff as a mannequin, his hands clasped in front of him. Suguro realized at once that this man knew nothing.

When the reception was over, Suguro and his wife walked through the deserted lobby of the hotel and went out in search of a taxi. As they passed through the door, his wife muttered as if to herself, 'What a relief for Yasuko.'

'Yes. She's got a full-time job now as a wife.' For such a mundane reply, his voice sounded a bit strained.

Then abruptly his wife said, 'Now everything will be all right . . . for you . . . and for us. . . .'

Suguro stopped and stole a quick glance back at her. For some reason that familiar smile slowly formed on his wife's face. She hurriedly climbed into the taxi that had stopped in front of them.

She knows everything. For a while the two sat side by side in the taxi without uttering a word. The smile had not melted from her lips. Suguro was unable to fathom the meaning of that smile. All he knew for sure was that his wife was not the sort of woman who would ever voice those feelings again. . . .

'Once this operation is over, everything will be all right. But you've been the real trooper, Yoshiko. . . . You've looked after him for three years now.' Yasuko turned towards the bed. 'Once you get out of the hospital, you must be especially good to your wife, or you'll be punished for it!'

'I'm already being punished,' Suguro mumbled, looking up at the ceiling. 'As you can see.'

'There, that's just what I'm talking about!' Yasuko's laugh was conspicuously loud. 'I'm always saying that to my husband, aren't I, dear? How hard all this has been on Yoshiko.'

'Not at all. I'm . . . totally insensitive to the whole thing.'

There were thorns and private meanings concealed beneath each of their remarks. But Yasuko's husband was bored, and he twiddled his thumbs on his lap. 'Don't you think we ought to be going?' he said. 'You shouldn't wear out a sick man.'

'You're right. I'm sorry. I had no idea. . . .'

Her casual remark pricked at Suguro's chest. It was a suitable end to their conversation. Yasuko's husband had 'no idea' what was going on. And the remaining three pretended to have 'no idea' what was happening, when in fact they merely refrained from saying anything out loud. They all behaved as though nothing had happened. For his sake. And for their own.

'Good morning. Good morning!' On the veranda, their son was still trying to teach the myna bird. 'Say it! Why won't you say it, birdie?'

4

Three days before the operation, the drab days were suddenly filled with activity. Nurses wheeled him off to measure the capacity and function of his lungs, and a score of blood samples were taken. They needed to know not only his blood type, but also how many minutes it would take his blood to coagulate when it began to flow from his body on the operating table.

It was early December. Since Christmas was approaching, from his room he could hear the choir from the nursing school practising carols during their lunch break. Each year on Christmas Eve the nurses sang carols for the children in the paediatrics ward.

'I suppose I should make the same preparations this time as for the other operations?' Suguro asked a young physician. An experienced surgeon would be wielding the scalpel of course, but this young doctor would be assisting.

'Well, you're an old hand at surgery now, Mr Suguro. There's really nothing you need to do to get ready.'

'They turned me into a boneless fillet of fish last time . . .' This was how patients referred to the extraction of ribs from the chest cavity. 'This time I guess I'm going to end up a one-winged airplane. . . .'

The young doctor smiled wryly and turned his head towards the window. The voices of the Christmas chorus flowed in annoyingly, singing a Japanese folk-song:

> A blast of the steam whistle,
> And already my train is leaving Shimbashi . . .

'What are my odds?' Suguro spat out the question, his eyes fixed on the doctor's face. 'What are my odds of surviving this next operation?'

'This is no time to get faint-hearted. You'll be just fine.'

'Are you sure?'

'Yes . . .' But there was a brief, painful moment of hesitation in the young doctor's voice. 'Of course I'm sure.'

> The mountains at Hakone
> Are an impregnable pass.
> Not even the impassable barrier at Han-yu
> Can compare . . .

I don't want to die. I don't want to die! No matter how painful this third operation is, I don't want to die yet. I still don't know what life means, what it is to be a human being. I'm idle and I'm lazy, and I go on deceiving myself. But, if nothing else, I have finally learned that when one person comes in contact with another, it is no simple encounter – there is always some sort of scar left behind.

If I had not come in contact with my wife, or with Yasuko, their lives might have turned out very differently.

Once the doctor had gone, Suguro turned to the myna bird, which had been moved from the veranda into his room, and whispered, 'I want to live . . . !' The newspaper at the bottom of the cage was covered with white droppings and strewn with half-eaten balls of feed. The bird hunched its black body and stared at him with those sorrowful eyes. The yellowish-brown beak reminded him of the foreign priest's nose. Its face, too, resembled the face of the tippling father.

I couldn't help what happened between Yasuko and me. And I had no choice but to go to that clinic. It wasn't a sin. It was just something that happened between Yasuko and me. But as a result, one ripple has expanded into two, and two ripples have grown into three. Everyone is covering up for everyone else. . . .

The myna bird cocked its head and listened silently to his words. Just as the priest seated in the confessional had wordlessly turned his ear to listen.

But then the bird leaped to the upper perch, wagged its behind, and dropped a round turd onto the floor of the cage.

Night came. The night nurse and a doctor began looking into each room. He could hear their footsteps in the distance.

'Everything all right?'

'Yes. Just fine.'

The light from their flashlight crept along the wall of his darkened room. There was a rustle of movement as the myna bird shifted inside its covered cage.

One ripple expands into two, then three. It was he who had first cast the stone, he who had created the first ripple. And if he died during this next operation, the ripples would likely spread out further and further. The actions of a human being are never self-contained. He had built up walls of deception around everyone, and initiated lies between three individuals that could never be obliterated. It was a deceit worse than glossing over the death of someone in a hospital.

Three more days until my operation. If I survive . . . I guess I'll be spending this coming January here in the hospital, too.

In January, Suguro would turn forty.

'At forty, I no longer suffered from perplexities . . .' Confucius once wrote.

He shut his eyes and tried to force himself to sleep.

5

The morning of his operation arrived. It was still dark in his room when the nurse awakened him. He had been given a sedative the night before, and his head was heavy.

6.30 a.m. The hair is shaved off his chest in preparation for surgery. 7.30 a.m. An enema is administered. 8 a.m. An injection and three pills are given for the first stage of anaesthesia.

Suguro's wife and her mother softly opened the door to his room. They peered inside, and one of them whispered, 'I don't think he's asleep yet . . .'

'Stupid! Do you think one shot is going to knock me out? I'm not a newcomer at this, you know.'

'You should try not to talk too much,' his mother-in-law said anxiously.

'Don't move around.'

Yasuko has probably even forgotten that I am having surgery today. With a hairclip poked in her hair like a brass fitting, she was probably heating up coffee for her public-servant husband right now.

Two young nurses came in pushing a wheeled bed. 'Well, let's go, Mr Suguro.'

'Just a minute.' He turned to his wife. 'Would you bring the birdcage in from the veranda? I suppose he's entitled to a goodbye, too.'

Everyone smiled at this jest.

'All right, all right.' His wife returned, carrying the birdcage. The bird peered out at Suguro with those penetrating eyes. *You're the only one who knows what I could not tell the old priest in the confessional. You listened to me, without even knowing what any of it meant.*

'I'm ready now.'

They lifted Suguro and laid him face-up on the bed. With a creak it started down the hallway. His wife walked alongside, pulling up the blanket that seemed ready to slide off.

'Ah, Mr Suguro. Keep smiling!' someone called after him.

They passed patients' rooms and nurses' stations on both sides, went by the kitchen, and into the elevator.

When the elevator stopped on the fifth floor, the bed gave a squeak and moved down the corridor, which reeked of disinfectant. The closed doors of the operating theatre lay just ahead.

'Well, Mrs Suguro. This is as far as you can go . . . ,' a nurse said.

Family members were not allowed to proceed any further.

Suguro looked up at his wife. That smile flickered again on her drawn face. That smile, which seemed to show up on any and all occasions.

In the operating theatre his gown was stripped from him and a blindfold was placed over his eyes. When he was shifted to the hard operating table, several hands hooked down the sheet that was thrown over his body. To facilitate the insertion of needles for the intravenous blood transfusions, hot towels were placed on his legs to distend the vessels. Near his ears he could hear the rattle of metal instruments being arranged.

'You know how this anaesthetic works, don't you?'

'Yes.'

'All right. I'm going to place the mask over your mouth.'

A smell of rubber filled his nostrils. The rubber mask covered his nose and mouth.

'Please count after me.'

'Yes.'

'One.'

'One.'

'Two.

'Two . . .'

His wife's face flashed across his mind. *She knows everything. Is she just waiting for everything to be quietly resolved? When did I drive her to such an extremity of self-deception . . . ?*

'. . . Five.'

'Five.'

Suguro fell into a deep sleep.

It seemed like only one or two minutes later when he opened his eyes. But it was after dark that same day before he slowly began to awaken from the anaesthetic.

Directly above him was the face of the young doctor. And his wife's smile.

'Well, hello there!' He tried to be droll, but immediately dropped back into a heavy sleep. It was nearly four in the morning when he awoke again.

'Well, hello there!' he tried a second time.

He could not see his wife. The grim-faced night nurse was wrapping the black cloth of a blood-pressure gauge around his right arm. The rubber hose of an oxygen inhalor was thrust into his nostril, and tubes from the plasma bottles trailed from his legs. There were two black holes in his left breast, vinyl tubes poking out from them. Through these tubes a noisy machine sucked the blood which was collecting in his chest cavity and siphoned it into a glass bottle. Suguro's throat was parched.

'Water . . . water, please.'

'You aren't allowed any.'

His wife tiptoed into the room with an ice-bag.

'Water, please.'

'You'll have to wait.'

'How long was I in surgery?'

'Six hours.'

He wanted to say, 'I'm sorry,' but he did not have the strength.

He felt as though enormous boulders had been stacked up on his chest. But he was accustomed to physical agony.

A pale streak of light illuminated the window. When he realized that dawn was near, he felt for the first time that he would survive. His luck had indeed been extraordinarily good. His joy was great.

However, he continued to spit up phlegm laced with blood. Normally, this blood would clear up within two or three days after surgery, evidence that the blood from the wound on the lung had thoroughly coagulated. But in Suguro's case, even after four or five days the thread of blood did not disappear from his spittle. And his fever would not subside.

Doctors filed one after another in and out of his room; out in the hallway they discussed his predicament in hushed tones. Suguro knew at once that they suspected a leak in his bronchi. If that were the case, various bacilli would cluster around the wound and complicate his condition with thoracic empyema. He would have to undergo surgery several more times. The doctors hastily commenced injections of antibiotics and began to administer ilotycin.

In the second week, the blood finally vanished from his phlegm and his fever gradually began to decline.

'I can tell you this now . . . ,' his surgeon smiled, sitting down on a chair next to Suguro's pillow. 'You just barely made it. This whole thing has been a dangerous feat of tightrope-walking.'

'During the operation, too?'

'Yes. In the middle of surgery your heart stopped for several seconds. That gave us a real scare. But your luck has held strong.'

'You must have accumulated many good deeds over the years, Mr Suguro,' laughed the young doctor, who stood off to one side.

After a month he was finally able to pull himself up, using the rope that hung over his bed. His legs had withered, and he was without seven ribs and one entire lung. He stroked his meagre body with his emaciated arms.

'Oh, say. What's happened to my myna bird?' he asked abruptly one day. During his long struggle with the disease, he had forgotten all about the bird. The nurses had agreed to look after it for him.

His wife lowered her eyes.

'It died.'

'How?'

'Well, after all, the nurses didn't have time to look after it. Neither did I. We fed it, but one really cold night we forgot to bring it back into the room. We shouldn't have left it out on the veranda all night.'

Suguro was silent for a few moments.

'I'm sorry. But I feel as though it took your place. . . . I buried it at home in the garden.'

He couldn't blame her. Certainly his wife had not had the leisure to fret over a bird.

'Where's the cage?'

'It's still out on the veranda.'

His head still swimming, he slid his feet into his slippers. Supporting himself with one hand on the wall, he made his way to the veranda, one step at a time. The dizziness eventually passed.

The sky was clear. Cars and buses raced along the road below. The wan summer sun trickled into the empty birdcage. The bird's white droppings clung to the perches; the water trough was dry and stained brown. There was a smell to the deserted cage. It was the smell of the bird, of course, but the smell of Suguro's own life was also a part of it. The breathy odour of the words he had spoken to the creature that had once lived inside this cage.

'Everything will be all right now,' his wife said as she held onto him to support him.

He started to say, 'No, it won't.' But he caught himself and said nothing.

DESPICABLE BASTARD

'Hey, what are you doing? You won't get away with that!'

He turned around in surprise. The supervisor they had nicknamed Centipede was standing behind him, hands thrust into the pockets of his work clothes.

'You may think you can slack off because nobody's looking, but I know what you're up to. I know!'

'I've got a headache.'

Egi, being a cowardly sort of person, blurted out the first excuse that came into his head.

He screwed up his face as though in pain and wiped his forehead with his hand, and strangely enough he began to believe that he actually did have a headache. The strength had gone out of his legs, and he staggered unsteadily.

The supervisor had walked on two or three steps when he turned around and studied Egi's movements with suspicious eyes. Then he came back and asked, 'Have you really got a fever?'

'Uh-huh,' Egi sighed.

'Then why didn't you say you were ill?' The supervisor knit his brows sullenly. 'You're hopeless. Go and report that you're leaving work early.'

Egi slipped out of the factory, avoiding the eyes of the other students. When he was outside, a sly smile appeared on his slender face. Caught up in the satisfaction of having eluded the normal eight hours of labour service and the pleasure of having outwitted his supervisor, he felt scarcely any guilt at leaving his classmates behind. He watched as a group of women from the volunteer corps, dressed in fatigues, came wearily towards him, dragging their shovels and straw baskets after digging an air-raid shelter. Even the sight of them did not fill him with the remorse of a deserter, and he went back to his dormitory in Shinano-machi.

The dormitory where Egi lived had been built by a Christian organization for the benefit of their members' children. Recently, however, many of the Christian students had been drafted or had otherwise withdrawn from the dorm, so unaffiliated students like Egi had been allowed to move in. Though it passed as a dormitory, the building was simply a brown-painted, two-storey wooden structure with no more than fifteen or sixteen rooms.

Egi realized that there would be nothing to do if he went back to his room, and that none of his dormmates would be back yet, so he made one of his rare visits to the Outer Gardens of the Meiji Shrine. He sat down on the grass and watched as a winter squall picked up scraps of straw and old newspapers and tossed them about. He extracted his aluminium lunch-pail from his knapsack, dejectedly took out the handful of rice that had been crammed into its corner, and slowly began to chew it.

As he worked his chopsticks, Egi thought vaguely about what would happen to him in the future. He had no idea what course the war would take. Of late he had not the slightest interest in whether Japan won or lost. His days were filled exclusively with hunger and the strain of having to work at a factory even though he was a student. It frightened him to think that one day he would be taken off to live in a barracks like so many of the senior students.

The winter sky was perpetually cloudy. From far in the distance he heard a dull roar, like the whirring of an airplane propeller. Two young nurses from the Keiō Hospital, laughing about something, came walking along the path at the edge of the lawn.

Egi set his lunch-box down and, thrusting his head forward like a baby tortoise, listened covetously to the nurses' sparkling voices. The laughter of young women, and the sight of white uniforms instead of work fatigues, seemed to have a freshness that was almost unbearable in contrast to his stifling daily existence.

'Hey!' A loud voice suddenly broke into Egi's thoughts. An NCO, dressed in a sweat-soaked military uniform with an arm-band reading 'Military Police', was standing in front of him, supporting his bicycle with his hand. 'Hey, what are you doing? Are you a student?'

Intimidated by the man's piercing gaze and the bony, square set of his jaw, Egi didn't reply. At the factory where he worked, there were often stories about military police catching and interrogating draft labourers and student workers who were shirking their duties.

'No answer, you bastard?' the officer said slowly. He leaned his bicycle against the trunk of a tree and, gripping his sword with his right hand, came up to Egi.

In a croaking voice Egi explained that he had left the factory early because of illness. 'I . . . I wasn't . . . wasn't . . . feeling well . . . ,' he stammered, his eyes fixed on the ground. But something in the way he stuttered gave the officer the impression that he was being mocked.

For an instant it felt to Egi as though his face had been hammered with a lead pipe. He cried out, covering his face with his hands.

'Make fun of me, will you, you bastard!' The officer began to kick Egi viciously. As the two nurses looked on in fear, Egi fell to his knees, his hands resting on the ground. The leather boots pounded into his knees and legs again and again.

'Forgive me, sir!' To quell the officer's wrath, Egi obsequiously employed military terminology. 'I am at fault. Please forgive me.'

The leather boots tramped off, but even after the bicycle had disappeared far down the road, Egi remained motionless on his hands and knees. He glanced around in search of his glasses, which had been hurled to the ground; they lay in a clump of yellowed grass, their frames bent. When he spotted them, the first waves of searing humiliation surged up from the pit of his stomach. The nurses still stood watching apprehensively from behind a tree. 'Go away!' Inwardly Egi pleaded with them. 'Please go away!'

He returned to the dorm, his legs throbbing. At the entrance, Iijima, a student from M. University, was removing his gaiters. Like Egi, Iijima was one of the students living at the dorm who was not a Christian. Egi was on the verge of telling him what had just happened to him, but fearing that Iijima would despise him, he said nothing.

'I'm starving to death.' Finished with military drills for the day, Iijima massaged his feet. 'They're damned stingy with their food at this "Amen" dormitory.'

'Yeah,' Egi nodded feebly.

'You going to Gotemba?'

'Gotemba? What for?'

'Haven't you heard?' Iijima, a burly member of the university karate team, folded his arms. 'Next week they're going to a leper hospital called Aioi-en. It's supposed to be a regular event at this dorm. I imagine one of the "Amen" boys like Ōsono came up with the idea. But why should we have to go along when we aren't one of the "Amens"?'

Egi left Iijima sitting in the entranceway and went to his room, where he stretched out on his bed. His knees had started to ache. Gingerly, he pulled up his trousers to find that a good deal of skin had been scraped off. The gash was saturated with blood. Studying the wound, he was filled with a seething anger that a military policeman virtually his own age could be capable of such violence. Why hadn't he fought back? Why hadn't he put up a struggle? But he knew that he had no pride, that he was the sort of man who would abandon all principle in the face of violence or the threat of physical harm. 'It's like an act of nature,' he muttered to himself. 'The more you try to resist, the worse off you are.'

He dozed until sundown. From time to time he opened his eyes a crack; the world outside the window was submerged beneath a grey evening haze. His room was cold, and his wounded knee hurt. He listened forlornly to the banging sounds from the next room, where Ōsono was shifting his desk around. Ōsono was a Christian, and had been at the dorm longer than anyone. He was a highly-strung, pallid-faced student at Tokyo University. And for some reason he seemed unable to rest unless he moved his desk to a new position every third day or so.

Egi finally woke up around dinner time. Favouring his swollen knee, he went downstairs to the cafeteria. The other students were silently eating the meagre helping of rice served to them in soup bowls. Ōsono stood by himself at the front of the room, reciting to the group from a history of the Japanese Christian martyrs. The founder of the dormitory had left instructions that the students were to say prayers each evening at dinner, and that the student on duty that night was to read a passage from some religious work.

Like all the others, Egi ate with a sullen look on his face. Recently the students were too exhausted from days filled by military drill and labour service at the factory to find the energy or the enthusiasm to talk to one another during meals.

'In this torture the hands and feet of the prisoners were lashed together with ropes, which were tied behind their backs. They were then suspended from the ceiling while the officers beat them with whips.' In a strained voice, Ōsono was reading from what seemed to be an account of Christian martyrdoms in Hiroshima Prefecture at the beginning of the Meiji era.

But no one in the room had any interest in the story. The non-Christians were of course apathetic, but even the believers were only pretending to listen out of a sense of duty.

'Despite being subjected to this torture, neither Kan'emon nor Mohei nor any of the other Christians of Nakano village would agree to apostatize. In fact, calling upon the Holy Mother, they expressed their thanks to God for granting them this trial.'

At this point Ōsono slammed the book shut. Then with a fraudulently pious gesture he crossed himself and dug into the soya beans and rice in his bowl. Egi stole a glance at Ōsono – that nervous face with the rimless glasses – and wondered if he was really interested in the sorts of things he had just been reading about. 'The whole book's a bunch of nonsense,' Iijima muttered from the next seat. Egi couldn't bring himself to agree, but it was obvious that every story Ōsono recited had to do with people who did not succumb to violence and torture. He recalled the blow to his face that afternoon, his entreaties as he knelt on the ground on all fours, his glasses knocked into the withered grass. He hated being so afraid of physical pain.

'You're lucky you weren't born into a Christian family. One blow, and you'd chuck your God just like that!' Iijima called out to Egi in a loud voice. His remark was made half in jest, but no one laughed. Egi thought of the ugly scene that morning, and his face stiffened.

Late that evening Egi pulled out his hotplate, warmed up some dried cuttlefish he had been sent from home, and ravenously gobbled it up. Electric hotplates were banned in the dormitory because they often overloaded the fuses, but he had hidden one away in his cupboard for times of need. Concerned that the delicious smell of the cuttlefish might leak outside his door and attract the attention of the other starving students, he opened his window half-way and aired his room after cooking each fish.

Through the wall he heard Ōsono leaving his room. The door creaked and then slammed shut.

'Probably going to the toilet.' Egi relaxed and, stretching out on his bed, slowly relished the taste of the cuttlefish in his mouth. But this was imprudent. Ōsono thrust his pale face round the door, his rimless glasses glittering. When he recognized the aroma in the room, his eyes flashed and he peered sternly at Egi.

'It's cuttlefish,' Egi mumbled timidly, unable to endure Ōsono's accusing stare. 'My family sent it to me.'

Without a word Ōsono thrust a slice of the fish between his thin, colourless lips. 'Yeah. Next Sunday we're all going to put on a programme at the Aioi-en in Gotemba. The round trip will cost five yen. I thought I'd let you know in advance.' His eyes never strayed from the tentacles of the cuttlefish that still lay on the hotplate. 'As you're new to the dorm, this will be your first time. We do this programme every year.'

Ōsono explained that the Christian organization which had founded the dormitory also managed the Aioi-en leper hospital. For that reason the students at the dorm put on a show for the Gotemba clinic once every year.

'I know you're not a Christian, but whether you are or not, you're a student at this dorm, so I knew you'd come along with us.'

'Is there anybody who isn't going?'

'That bastard . . . er, Iijima was reluctant at first, but he agreed to go after I told him I'd report him to the dorm supervisor.'

After Ōsono had left the room, Egi began to worry. He had no real knowledge about leprosy, but during his childhood he had been vaguely frightened of the disease. A beggar with twisted fingers had occasionally come begging with a frail voice around the streets of his village. Each time, his grandmother would quickly hide him in the linen closet. In his middle-school years he had passed through a period when he was virtually paranoid about the disease. This was the result of his reading an adult amusement magazine that featured photographs of gruesome skeletons and descriptions of the various symptoms of leprosy.

'It's supposed to be contagious if you have any kind of open wound on your body . . .' Gingerly, he pulled up his trouser leg. The injured knee, which he had just bandaged, felt hot and was beginning to swell. 'I wonder if I can beg off because of this,' he pondered aloud. On the other hand, he didn't like the thought of being called self-centred by Ōsono and the other Christians. 'If I go, I'll keep as far away from the patients as I can.'

As he made this resolution, Egi thought what a contemptible specimen of humanity he was. To visit a hospital and then try to avoid the patients out of a loathing for them – he knew full well how despicable that would be. But his fear of infection and his dread of physical pain still took precedence over everything else.

On Sunday morning Egi and the other students from the dormitory boarded the train for Gotemba at Tokyo Station. The train had arrived at the station only thirty minutes before, but already it was packed beyond capacity. Men dressed in patriotic uniforms with rucksacks on their laps, and women dressed in work pantaloons and carrying parcels of scavenged food had spread newspapers on the floor between the seats of the carriage and were jamming corridors.

On the platform one or two scraggy circles of patriots were croaking out military songs, but none of the passengers or the people scurrying along the platform paid the slightest attention to them. The dorm students were the only ones who paused at the door of the train to look at these ceremonies for recruits going off to the front. The thought crossed their minds that soon they too would stand on a station platform, their faces tense, while a circle of well-wishers clustered around them. Then, realizing that each of them was thinking the same thing, they abruptly lowered their eyes.

As they had left the dormitory and headed for the station, and now as they waited for the train to depart, the students had split into two groups – those who were Christians, and those like Iijima and Egi who were not. Sometimes the Christian students would glance back at Iijima, who had made his disapproval of this day-trip a matter of public record, and then whisper among themselves.

'Look at him now – Ōsono's enough to make you sick.' Iijima crouched down on the train step and spat loudly. Egi climbed on the step and looked down the platform. Ōsono had joined one of the groups surrounding a new recruit; he was clapping his hands and singing the war song. Seeing this hypocritical behaviour, Egi had to agree that Ōsono was something of a phoney.

When the packed train jerked to a start, Iijima again spat onto the tracks, then turned to Ōsono, who was standing beside him. 'It's a sorry fellow who has his circle and gets sent off to war only to come skulking right back, isn't it, Ōsono?' he asked lightly. His sarcasm was directed straight at Ōsono, who had been conscripted into a student division the previous year and been sent off with a great flurry, only to return ignominiously to the dormitory the very next day. Ōsono's nervous face turned red.

Leaning against the door to the lavatory, Egi tried to imagine the day when he would be given such a send-off. Life in boot camp would begin for him. Every day he would be beaten in the dark barracks room. At the thought of the pain his body would have to endure, Egi's chest constricted. Once again he thought of himself a week before, on his hands and knees in the Outer Garden, shamelessly pleading, 'I am at fault. Please forgive me.' 'That's just how it'll be if I end up in the army,' he thought. 'I'll gladly abandon all sense of self-esteem out of fear of being beaten. That's the kind of person I am.'

'Physical pain affects me more than mental torment,' he thought as his body swayed with the movement of the train. 'That's why I would abandon all pride and all conviction.'

Three hours later the train arrived in Gotemba. The sky was dark with clouds as they disembarked. Apparently word of their arrival time had been sent ahead; a middle-aged man dressed in a white smock was waiting beyond the ticket gate, a smile on his face.

'Welcome, welcome!' He bowed his head to the students, then identified himself as an officer worker at the Aioi-en. 'Our patients have been looking forward to this day for an entire month.'

The square in front of the station was deserted. Shops that had once sold souvenirs stood with their doors ajar, and not a sound could be heard from within. A single charcoal-burning bus awaited the group. It was held together with chewing-gum and spittle, the man explained with a smile. As they entered the bus, the odour of disinfectant stabbed at their noses.

When Egi smelled the disinfectant, the anxiety and fear, which had totally fled his mind, came flooding back. Perhaps a flock of patients had been sitting on these seats. Egi hurriedly covered his knee with his hand. The bus set off, rocking back and forth, and clattered along the streets. As it made its way along roads lined with pine trees, kicking up clouds of white dust, Egi began to be bothered by a pain in his knee that he had not noticed on the train. When he had checked the wound before leaving the dormitory that morning, a white layer of skin had begun to grow over it, but it still hadn't really begun to heal. It was possible that he might pick up some bacteria today at the Aioi-en. He looked apprehensively around the bus, noticing the cracked leather of the seats and the dust-coated windows.

Ōsono stood up in the aisle and suggested that the group sing a hymn. With a solemn look on his face, he raised his hand above his head and called, 'Ready – one, two, three.'

> 'O come all ye faithful,
> Joyful and triumphant,
> O come ye, O come ye to Bethlehem.
> Come and behold him,
> Born the king of angels.

'Humph. Conceited slobs,' Iijima fumed from the seat behind Egi.

Egi turned round and whispered, 'Iijima, do you think we'll be all right?'

'Huh?'

'Do you think we'll get infected?'

'How should I know?' Iijima looked away. 'I can't stomach the zeal for charity they have at this dormitory.'

'How nice it would be if I could be as decisive about everything as Iijima is,' thought Egi. He looked vacantly out of the dusty window as farmhouses and fields whisked by. 'If it wasn't for this wound,' he told himself, 'even I could feel good about going to the hospital.'

He was disgusted with himself for being afraid of the patients at the Aioi-en. The same craven spirit that had impelled him to betray his own feelings and beg forgiveness from the MP a week earlier still had him in its grip. No matter how priggish and hypocritical Ōsono's attitude might be, the fellow had a strength he himself could never hope to emulate. He could not share Iijima's contempt for the Christian students.

The bus finally plodded its way out of the forest. In spite of the cloudy sky, faint rays from the afternoon sun had made the tree trunks glimmer a silver colour. There was no longer a house to be seen. The Aioi-en had been built in a region far away from any human settlements.

A wooden building with a red roof appeared beyond the trees. Two men dressed in white coats stood at the doorway waving their hands at the bus.

'Here we are!' called the staff worker, who was sitting next to the bus driver. They had arrived at the Aioi-en.

As he climbed off the bus, Egi looked about nervously to see if there were any patients walking around near him. But he could see no sign of anyone who might be a patient in the vicinity of the building.

Instinctively, Egi tried to stay close to Iijima. He felt more capable of making excuses and apologies for himself if he was with Iijima than if he mingled with the Christian students. But Iijima thrust his hands into the pockets of his tattered overcoat, spat on the ground and walked away from him.

The red-roofed building was the hospital's administrative office. In the reception room the students were given plates piled high with steamed potatoes and cups of muddy tea. They gnawed like dogs on the potatoes.

Smiling broadly, an old man dressed in a suit came into the room. 'Unfortunately our hospital director had to be in Shizuoka today. My name is Satō, and I work here in the office. Thank you all for coming.' Then, with one missing tooth leaving a gap in his smile, the chubby old man explained that the patients had been eagerly awaiting this visit for over a month. 'Each one of our patients has saved a potato from their own rations to give to you.'

At this announcement, the students stopped chewing and the room fell silent.

'The patients have been waiting in the assembly hall for a half an hour already. They really are looking forward to your programme. Would you like to be disinfected before you go into the auditorium? I doubt whether anyone will be infected, but, well, you might feel more at ease.'

Egi and two or three others were about to get up from their chairs when Ōsono turned on them indignantly. 'If you have any regard for the goodwill these patients have shown us, you won't need disinfecting.'

'Well, well.' The old man seemed a little taken aback at Ōsono's agitation. 'Of course, the disinfecting really doesn't have much effect . . .'

There was a chilly silence. Egi stared in bewilderment at his trouser knee and at the plate of steamed potatoes. Then he raised his head and looked around for Iijima. His friend was standing with his arms folded, gazing petulantly at the ceiling.

'Well, shall we be going?' the old man said awkwardly.

Led by Satō and a young nurse, the students crossed the courtyard and headed towards the hospital building. The overcast sky seemed ready to release more rain at any moment. The infirmary was a long, narrow wooden structure of three storeys; with its peeling paint it looked very much like an old army barracks. To one side was a large playing field, possibly an exercise ground. Beyond this, fields of red earth, cultivated by the patients with only a mild case of the disease, stretched out beneath the slate-grey sky.

To Egi, it seemed a dark, depressing landscape. The patients suffering from Hansen's disease would never be able to leave this narrow space and venture into the world outside. Forsaken by their families and by society at large, they had no alternative but to die here. The thought filled Egi with an emotion somewhere between compassion and grief. But then his coat brushed against a wall of the infirmary and he quickly recoiled.

The auditorium was a hall large enough to accommodate about a hundred straw mats. It had a crudely constructed platform that served as a stage. Satō explained that the more able patients came here to listen to motivational lectures and to put on a monthly show.

'Last month they dramatized the dialogue between Jesus and Mary

Magdalene,' the old man announced. 'Some of the patients are very good at that sort of thing. It was a great success.'

'We can't put on anything that impressive,' said Ōsono, blushing and nodding his head. 'But we'll do our best.'

The other students held their breath as they climbed the stairs to the dressing-room, which reeked of disinfectant. A black curtain hung between the stage door and the hall, so they could not get a glimpse of the assembled patients. But Egi estimated from the number of coughs and snorts that there must be about eighty patients waiting out there.

Anxiety gradually tightened its grip on Egi's chest. For whatever reason, since they had arrived here his wound had begun to ache more than ever. The thought that bacteria might already have got to him from somewhere made him even more resentful of Ōsono for refusing the disinfectant.

In the dressing-room, they heard a smattering of applause when Satō climbed onto the stage. Iijima located a tiny rip in the black curtain and peeped out at the audience, then turned to Egi with a sullen look.

'Look through here. There's swarms of them out there!'

There was more sparse applause, and Satō came back to the dressing-room. 'Well, it's all yours!'

As if they had planned it at some point, Ōsono led out about five of the Christian students and leaped up the stairs.

This time the applause was loud. When it ended, Ōsono gave the lead in his girlish voice, 'One, two, three.'

While the group sang hymns for the patients, the non-Christians listened in glum silence. Even if they had wanted to sing something just to spite Ōsono and his group, there weren't any songs that they all knew. It became evident that the Christian group had secretly been practising for some time in an effort to demonstrate something or other to the non-believers. When the chorus broke off, a literature student from Tokyo University named Hamada sang a German *lied*. Then in an excited voice Ōsono cried, 'I'd like to recite a poem for you all.' His voice trembled as he began.

> 'Life in this world is a path of pain.
> No matter what trials I encounter,
> Until the very moment of death . . .'

'A poem? Hah! He calls that a poem?' In exasperation Iijima opened the dressing-room window and spat. 'Is that supposed to cheer up the patients?'

Hesitantly, Egi brought his eye up to the hole in the curtain. And had his first look at the patients he feared so much.

The hall was dark, so he could not clearly distinguish the individual faces of the patients. Just as he had thought, the majority of them seemed to be middle-aged men. But as his eyes grew accustomed to the faint light, he noticed among the balding men several young women dressed in *meisen* silk kimonos or white aprons. They kept their hands on their laps and tilted their heads to listen to the performance. Egi looked towards the back of the auditorium. Several stretchers had been lined up in the back row; patients with advanced cases of leprosy lay with white cloths wrapped around their faces, listening to Ōsono's poem.

'Life in this world is a path of pain.
No matter what trials I encounter,
Until the very moment of death
I will continue to tread that path.'

Egi of course had no idea who had composed the poem. And he did not know why Ōsono had deliberately selected such a disquieting verse for this occasion. Except for intermittent coughs from various corners of the room, the auditorium was hushed. As the long poem continued, several women with balding heads dabbed at their eyes with handkerchiefs or the corners of their blankets.

'Iijima . . . ,' Egi said abruptly. 'Why don't we do something for the group?'

'Us?' A mocking smile crossed his lips. Then, careful not to be seen by Satō and the other students who were watching the stage from the dressing-room, Iijima twisted the fingers of his hand into a gnarled claw. 'Even if we end up like this?'

Again Egi thought of the gash on his knee and the white membrane of skin that veiled it. He threw open the dressing-room door and hurried outside. A dark, oppressive silence hung over the deserted exercise ground and the fields blanketed with rain-clouds. Far in the distance he could hear the faint sound of a train passing through Gotemba. 'You're a despicable bastard,' he wanted to shout at himself. 'A wretched, disgusting, despicable bastard!'

The Christian students' programme finished some thirty minutes later. Egi looked on from a window facing the courtyard until every last one of the patients had left the assembly hall. First the women retired, then the male patients. Many of them limped or walked with canes. Finally the most seriously afflicted were carried out on stretchers by their more able comrades. Those not on stretchers were carried on the shoulders of their friends.

Satō led the students back to the reception room, where they were treated to milk and bread with jam, items that were hard to come by in Tokyo. Iijima, who stared at the wall of the room as he gnawed on his bread, suddenly asked the old administrator, 'Do they play baseball here?' A framed photograph on the wall, depicting several patients dressed in uniforms and carrying bats standing beside two or three nurses, had prompted his question.

'They certainly do. Of course, it's just the healthier ones.' Satō smiled his toothless smile. 'I don't know anything about baseball myself, but I understand they're very good at it.'

'Hey, Ōsono!' Iijima called to Ōsono, whose face was still flushed from the excitement of the performance. 'Why don't you guys have a game of baseball with the team here?'

This was clearly Iijima's spiteful way of mocking the Christian students. Anybody – Iijima's words implied – can be philanthropic if all you have to do is stand up on a stage and look down at the inmates and sing songs and recite poetry; but why don't you have a go at baseball, where you'll actually have to come into physical contact with them?

'Why shouldn't we play? How about it, everybody?' Ōsono took up the challenge. 'Mr Satō, can you lend us some gloves?'

'We do have some the staff members use.' Once again the old man did his best to smooth over a delicate situation. 'You know, you really don't have to do this.'

Ōsono stood up, and the rest of the Christian students followed him reluctantly. Some nurses, oblivious to what was going on, cheerfully brought in some mitts and gloves and then scurried over to the infirmary to tell the patients about the game.

When they reached the playing field, the students put on their borrowed gloves and grudgingly began tossing the ball back and forth. Somehow their throws lacked vitality. A chilly breeze blew in from the direction of the fields.

'Hey, Egi!' Ōsono turned unexpectedly and called out. 'Come and play with us.'

He flung an extra glove at Egi. Egi cast a quick, pained look in Iijima's direction, but his friend was standing with his back to the group, staring at the fields with his hands thrust into his overcoat pockets.

A cheer rang out from the infirmary. Patients of both sexes were pressing their faces against every window, waving their hands or white handkerchiefs. The hospital team had just come running out of the infirmary, dressed in mud-stained uniforms.

At first glance, the patients looked no different from normal, healthy people. But when they lined up in front of the students and politely removed their caps to bow and say 'Thank you', Egi noticed that some of them had bald patches the size of large coins on the tops of their heads, while the lips of others were cruelly twisted out of shape.

Standing in the outfield, Egi shut his eyes and tried to recall the scene he had witnessed in the assembly hall. The terminal patients, lying back with white cloths wrapped around their faces, listening to Ōsono's clumsy poetry recitation; their companions who carried them on their backs when it was all over. The women and young girls who sat with drooping heads, their hands resting neatly on their laps. And Egi himself, who had tried to turn his back on all of them. 'You rotten bastard. You worthless, contemptible wretch.' The words formed again inside his mouth. He struggled to exorcize the image of his wounded knee as it flickered before his eyes.

The game proceeded. The students' turn at fielding ended, and somehow they had managed to hold off the patients' attack and keep them scoreless. Their opponents were more formidable than they had expected.

'Egi, you're up to bat next,' someone called. From the corner of his eyes, Egi saw a thin, derisive smile appear on the lips of Iijima, who was watching the game just off to one side.

When Egi picked up his bat and started for the plate, Iijima walked up beside him, as though he were going to suggest a batting strategy.

'Hey, Egi,' Iijima whispered perversely, his breath smelling foul. 'You're afraid, aren't you? You're going to get infected!'

Egi resolutely swung his bat. It connected firmly, and the white ball went sailing into the distance. 'Run!' someone shouted. Frantically, Egi rounded first base and continued running, but the first baseman had already caught the ball from the third and had started after Egi. Caught between two bases, Egi suddenly realized that the hand that would touch him with the ball belonged to a leper. He stopped dead in his tracks. 'Keep going!' he told himself, and sprinted off again. The first baseman threw the ball to the second baseman. When he got a close-up view of the second baseman's receding hairline and gnarled lips, Egi's body was no longer willing to respond to the promptings of his conscience. He stopped, hoping to be able to dodge his opponent, and looked up nervously at the approaching patient.

In the patient's eyes Egi saw a plaintive flicker, like the look in the eyes of an abused animal.

'Go ahead. I won't touch you,' the patient said softly.

Egi felt like crying when he was finally by himself. He stared vacantly at the infirmary, which now looked somehow like a livestock shed, and at the silver fields beneath the overcast sky. And he thought, 'Thanks to my fear of physical pain, I'll probably go on betraying my own soul, betraying love, betraying others. I'm a good-for-nothing, a wretch . . . a base, cowardly, vile, despicable bastard.'

MY BELONGINGS

He studied his wife as she crouched down and stoked the tiny furnace that heated their bath. Such a weary-looking face, he thought. Red shadows danced on her cheeks, and on the eyelids slightly puffy from the heat of the flames. Just yesterday afternoon, when Mita had announced his unexpected decision, Suguro had wondered all the more why he had ever married this woman. Outside it was raining – for three days now the rain had been soaking the roots of the *yatsude* in the garden. Since they could not put their clothes out to dry, their child's underwear and pyjamas were hanging in the bathroom and the hallway. The dankness and the unpleasant smell reminded the middle-aged Suguro of his own wrung-out marriage.

'Dad, I'm bored,' his son badgered him. 'Tell me a story.'

'All right. What would you like to hear about?'

He tilted his head, peering out of the window at the landscape held captive by the rain. This brand-new house. Forty minutes from downtown Tokyo, it stood on land carved out of the hillside. The hills, blanketed with groves of chestnut and lacquer trees, were cluttered now with tiny ready-built homes that rested on top of the red clay. For three days now the rain had been soaking these trees.

'One day some children were playing baseball near that grove of trees. The ball went into the trees, and the kids peered into the grove as they scrambled through the grass looking for it. And then . . .'

'And then – what happened?'

'And then . . .' Feeling rather cantankerous, Suguro pressed ahead. 'And then they found a man, about your father's age, hanging by his neck from one of the trees. His two unwashed legs dangled down from his faded nightshirt.'

Closing the furnace door, his wife muttered angrily, 'Don't tell him stories like that.'

'Why did he hang himself? This man, who was so much like your father, hadn't done anything particularly bad. He hadn't failed in his business. He hadn't fought with his wife. So nobody knew why he hanged himself. . . . But there was a dog that peered into the grove of trees with mournful eyes.'

'A dog?'

'That's right. The End.'

'What? That's the end? Stupid story!'

Suguro hugged his knees. I'll never leave this wife and child of mine, he thought. His own parents had grown to hate each other and were divorced; but in all likelihood he would spend his entire life beside this woman with the fat body and the exhausted face. He had this feeling primarily because her look of weariness sometimes overlapped in his mind with the face of 'that Man'. I suppose I will never abandon Him, either. Just as I will not desert my wife, I will not desert that Man, whose eyes have a look as sorrowful as those of the dog that peered into the forest.

The day before – a rainy day like this one – Suguro had sat in a crowded Shinjuku jazz café and talked about that Man with Mita. Young office workers and students sat huddled close to their girl-friends in chairs lined up like seats in a second-class railway car. Suguro and Mita were the only men sitting together, but it was the only place they could find to talk. The springs in their chairs were slack, and the cushions were still warm from the man and woman who had just occupied them.

'What did you want to tell me?'

'Next month I . . .' Mita shut his eyes, stroking the handle of his umbrella with the fingers of one hand. There was a lump on the lower part of his right cheek, like a tea-bag. Mita told everyone that it was a harmless sarcoma. But the presence of this clump of flesh made the nickname of 'Horse' that his friends had bestowed upon him seem all the more appropriate.

'Noisy in here, isn't it?'

'That's because it's Saturday.'

'Anyway, you were going to tell me . . . ?'

'I've decided to be baptized next month.'

With these words, Mita lowered his eyes to his glass of juice and blushed like a boy who has just removed his underpants in front of a doctor. Both men were novelists just a heartbeat away from their fortieth birthdays. Over the many years they had been friends they had tried in their fiction to probe one another's minds, but they had never exposed their feelings to each other face to face. There was something embarrassing about affording someone else an unobstructed view of your innermost emotions. Not even in their stories had they been able to display themselves totally unadorned beneath the light of the sun. They had been able to describe no more than the faintly discerned regions of the human heart, which were as difficult to grasp as droplets of water seeping through a bamboo basket.

'What? Baptized?'

'Uh-huh.'

Mita's wife had been a Christian for a long while, but he himself had persistently refused to consider conversion. Suguro had been baptized as a child, which probably explained why Mita had confided his decision to him.

But Suguro detested words like 'faith' and 'baptism'. They reeked of insincerity and naïveté, like hybrid second-generation names such as 'John' Kobayashi or 'Henry' Yamada. Moreover, there was something callous about using those words; it was as if you had nonchalantly opened up your soul to others. At some point Suguro had even stopped uttering the amorphous word 'God' and started looking for a different term to employ. A word that would have more substance for him. But he could not think of a Japanese phrase other than 'that Man' which he could use without blanching. From Suguro's childhood, 'that Man' had grown up within him. At present, just as Suguro had the sunken, grizzled face of a weary middle-aged man, that Man's face too was wan and tired and middle-aged. Suguro could scarcely call such a Man by the lifeless, abstract name 'God'.

'Why the sudden change of heart?'

In other words, what made you believe in God? – he realized the effrontery of his straightforward question. At the next table, a student had his fingers intertwined with those of a girl with bleached hair. When she tried to lean against him, he pulled away in embarrassment. The conversations at the tables behind them included snatches like: 'Well, after all, it really does make me mad.' 'Have you seen the movie *The Boss's Foreign Vacation*?' 'You're such an idiot!'

There was a loud crash, as though a waiter had dropped a tray of glasses, and everyone turned around to look. The café was filled with tobacco smoke and the smell of damp shoe leather; somehow it seemed an inappropriate place to be discussing the existence of God. And yet – yes! The throngs of Shinjuku visible through the window . . . the buses and cars waiting for the traffic signal to change . . . the advertisements for electric washing-machines. If the existence of God – of that Man – cannot be found along these dirty, commonplace Japanese streets, then why have you been writing stories? Suguro asked himself.

'Why? It's hard to explain.' Mita tried to put into words the motives behind his decision to be baptized. Six months earlier, when he had travelled to Rome with his wife, they had visited the Vatican. The incredibly gaudy buildings and piazzas had depressed him. When they went to Jerusalem, he was irritated to find that it had become as commercialized as the Zenkōji Temple in Nagano. But would he be depressed or irritated by things that mattered nothing to him, things that he had not come to love? He had ruminated over this question during the long plane journey from India to Haneda Airport.

'That's all there is to it?' Suguro laughed. 'That's a terribly mundane story, you know.'

'Yeah. Sorry I couldn't come up with a better one.'

Suguro knew of course that it was impossible to explain the well springs of faith to an outsider. The motives that Mita, blinking his eyes on his horse-like face, had expressed had been merely one chunk of ice from the great glacier that lay in the deepest recesses of his heart. A thick shell, like the dusty bark of a pine tree, clings to the outer skin of the consciousness until a person opens up to God. When that bark is peeled away, a white sap flows out. But it is impossible to talk about what it is that draws the sap to the surface. Mita could have said anything at all. Suguro had the feeling he would have understood if Mita had simply said he had been converted because the sky was blue when he woke up that morning.

'I envy you. You and Nagao.'

'What do you mean?'

'Both of you made this decision for yourselves.'

Nagao was another novelist nearing the age of forty. Several years earlier, when Nagao's wife began having emotional problems, the two of them had returned to their home town on an island at the very tip of the Japanese archipelago. Suguro had not heard why Nagao had been converted. But from reading his stories, Suguro knew that Nagao, scissored as he was between a pathologically demented wife and sickly children, had no choice but to cling frantically to them. He had settled into that life, and rather than flee from it, he had determined to endure it for the rest of his days. To bear his burden, he had needed some sense of meaning in his life. Or rather, he had accepted his life because it had meaning. In any case, Nagao, like Mita, had chosen a life of faith of his own volition.

From time to time the chestnut and lacquer trees in the grove would shudder and shake off muddy drops of rain, and the sound of it could be heard in Suguro's house. Mita and Nagao had chosen for themselves, but Suguro had not picked his faith through his own agency. That had long been his private burden. No – it was more than that. Although he had been only a child, Suguro had accepted the waters of baptism without a shred of faith. He still had a photograph taken of himself then. His skin had been dark in colour, and he poked his head forward and spoke in a peculiar voice, so everyone called him Crow. In the photograph, he was looking at the camera with apprehension in his eyes.

He could remember when he and his mother and sister set sail from Dairen, bound for Moji. The entire ship reeked of paint and the smell of yellow pickles coming from the kitchen; from the portholes he could see the black surface of the China Sea bobbing up and down, baring its white-fanged waves.

'Crow, Mother says we're going to stay with Uncle in Kobe! Oh dear! I've got another hole in these socks.'

His guileless sister thrust her worn socks in front of Suguro's face. She chattered gleefully about the life that awaited them.

'It will be wonderful, won't it, Mother?'

They were scheduled to arrive in Moji the following day, but their seasick mother had wrapped herself in a blanket and shut her eyes in agony. Gaping out the porthole at the dark, windswept ocean, Crow thought about his father back in Dairen, and about the black Manchu dog he had left behind. He needed no one to tell him that his father and mother had formally separated. His mother had explained to him and his sister that their father would eventually be returning to Japan too, but Crow knew at once from the movement of her eyes that she was lying. The chains that clamped the beds together during rough weather rattled. With that noise in his ears, Crow laid a picture-postcard of the ship on his lap and, using a coloured pencil, started writing to his school friends. But half-way through he tore the card to pieces. He would never be going back to Dairen to see them again.

As the train sped between Moji and Kobe, Crow stared intently out of the window; it was the first Japanese landscape he had ever seen. He was accustomed to seeing only kaoliang fields and mud farmhouses, so the thatched roofs and red persimmons all seemed new and exciting to him.

The family imposed themselves on his mother's sister. His uncle was a doctor at a hospital near their house. The couple had no children, so the place seemed as sterile as a clinic, and the smell of antiseptic seeped all the way in to the kitchen. Crow thought it strange that each room in the tiny house had a cross hanging on the wall.

His aunt and uncle were both members of the Catholic Church.

Uncle was a taciturn, expressionless man. He never uttered a word of complaint that his wife's sister and her children had invaded his house. But when he returned home from the hospital each night, he gave his sister-in-law and her children a cool glance and did not speak to them. This was his way of letting his wife know how he felt. In an effort to get on his good side, Crow's mother would suddenly feign cheerfulness, asking him if had had a busy day, or enquiring about his patients. He would not even smile in response, and merely grunted his answers. When dinner was finished he spread a medical journal out on his lap and read it in silence.

Even with his youthful comprehension of things, Crow had the vague notion that his uncle disliked them. As he leaned against the window frame and gazed out at the faint sun of late autumn trickling down on the Rokko hills, Crow thought about their house in Dairen, and then of the nights they had bumped along the snowy road in a horse-drawn carriage. He did not have the slightest idea what he should be doing for himself or his mother in their present circumstances.

He thought perhaps he should try to humour his peevish uncle by engaging him in conversation. But he was at a loss for what to say.

'Uncle, what's that?' Crow's sister was the one who pointed boldly at the cross nailed to the wall in the parlour. She had of course seen such objects in the Russian churches in Dairen, so she likely knew what they were.

'A cross,' Uncle answered crisply, looking up from his journal.

'What's it for?' This time Crow plunged into the conversation. But he could not purr like his sister.

His uncle snorted as though annoyed, and did not look up. Quickly his aunt intervened. 'Shin-chan, haven't you ever been to church? Church is where God is . . .'

Crow nodded at his aunt's lengthy explanation, but he didn't believe any of it. He thought of the old Russian who had sold holy images and medallions on the streets of Dairen. The old man's eyes always welled up with tears, and he was constantly wiping his nose with a filthy handkerchief. Crow and his friends had often thrown stones at him.

Each evening without fail Crow's mother had something to complain about to her sister and brother-in-law. At some point Uncle would suddenly stand up with a disagreeable look and leave the room. The air would turn chilly. In confusion Crow's aunt would say, 'Why don't you and your children go to bed now?' and hurriedly follow after her husband. When the mother and her two children had crawled into bed in their tiny upstairs room, Crow lay beside his snoring sister and took his turn listening to his mother's complaints.

'You just can't depend on relatives. Even a sister's no good once she's married off.'

'Mother, you say the same things to them every night. I'd get tired of hearing it if that was me. Why don't we find our own place to rent?'

They could hardly go on forcing themselves on this household indefinitely. His aunt was prevailing upon friends and acquaintances to find her sister a job. The only skill his mother possessed was playing the piano. She needed to stay on good terms with her sister and brother-in-law at least until she had found a position. To that end, when Crow came home from school each day he tried to ingratiate himself by volunteering to sweep the garden or help his aunt with her chores. But in his clumsy way, he managed to break the broom as he swept, and lost a *furoshiki* bundle when she sent him out on an errand.

On Sundays his aunt went to church for Mass. Sometimes her husband accompanied her. Aunt once invited her sister to come along. But the moment they returned home from Mass, Crow's mother started massaging her shoulders, muttering, 'Oh, I'm stiff. I couldn't tell whether those people had come to pray or to show off their fancy clothes.'

'But, Mother,' Crow responded, 'I think we ought to go to church. It would make Aunt happy.' Since leaving Dairen, the absence of his father had turned Crow into his mother's consultant. At such times he was able to express himself like a grown-up.

'Then you go with Sakiko. I'm not interested in licking their boots.'

'There you go again.'

The next Sunday he made up his mind and went out to the entrance-way where his aunt and uncle were putting on their shoes. But the words stuck in his throat. His uncle stared at him questioningly. Crow turned to his sister with a look of entreaty.

'Can we go to church with you?' she ventured.

'You want to come, Saki-chan?' With a sidelong glance at her husband, Aunt tried to sound pleased. 'And Shin-chan too?'

The two children walked silently beside their aunt, several paces behind their uncle. They took the Hankyū-line train to Shukugawa Station. This town had the only Catholic church in the region outside Kobe.

Crow's first Mass was a tedious, humiliating experience. The people around him kept springing to their feet or falling to their knees without warning. At his aunt's insistence, Crow had sat in the children's section of the congregation, where he had to imitate the movements of the younger children who clustered around him like baby monkeys. He stood staring into space while the other children recited the prayers they had memorized. He hadn't had enough sleep, and the sunlight streaming through the windows gave him a headache. When the perfume from the censer began to fill the nave, Crow felt as though he were going to vomit.

When he finally escaped outside an hour later, his face was pale and drained of blood.

'How did you like that?' But he could not answer his aunt's question.

With her customary feigned innocence, Sakiko gave a reply that delighted her aunt. 'I prayed as hard as I could!'

'How about you, Shin-chan?'.

Again his sister interjected in a melodic voice, 'I want to come to church again next week.'

As they made their way down the slope leading from the church to the railway station, Crow's uncle was suddenly walking beside him, and in a voice gentler than he had ever used before, he said, 'You didn't enjoy that, did you?'

Thereafter Crow was escorted to church every Sunday by his aunt. He went along, knowing he would incur her disfavour if he slackened off. And he had the feeling that his mother's standing in the household would disintegrate if he didn't go.

At the end of his fourth Mass at the church, Aunt took him to meet the old priest, who was dressed all in black. Crow was reminded of the sleepy-eyed old Russian in Dairen who sold icons on the streets and then huddled beneath an acacia tree to count the copper coins he had earned.

'Well, well,' the old priest smiled and placed his hand on Crow's shoulder. 'From now on you must come to the children's catechism class every Sunday. You'll make lots of friends there.'

'Shin-chan, what would you like to do?'

Crow looked up at his aunt. Aloud she seemed to be soliciting his opinion, but her face was clearly urging him to be quick about thanking the old priest.

Once the matter was settled, she said, 'I'm so happy for you, Shin-chan.'

His mother had nothing particular to say when she heard the news.

Apparently she had no objection to Crow attending catechism classes. So Crow and his sister joined five or six younger schoolchildren; a Japanese nun made them memorize phrases from a tiny book. It was full of phrases that meant absolutely nothing to Crow – 'The Holy Spirit', 'The Trinity'.

The day of their baptism was not long in coming. Crow was made to stand in the very front row of the sanctuary. He was surrounded by girls dressed in white with garlands of flowers in their hair, and boys in sailor outfits. Formal oaths were pledged before the actual ceremony of baptism was performed.

'Do you believe in the one and only God?' Before the entire congregation the old priest repeated the dialogue he had gone over with the children the day before, as though he were rehearsing them for a play performance.

'I believe,' Sakiko answered in a loud voice.

The priest turned to Crow and peered at him through his thick glasses. 'Do you believe in the one and only God?'

'I believe,' he replied.

As he studied his wife's bloated face beside the furnace, Suguro remembered something that a sharp-tongued colleague had said about her before the marriage.

'She's got a face like a puffy rice-ball!'

That rice-ball was now drab and lacklustre, and the once-slender body was grossly overfed. Her heart was weak, and from time to time she would wheeze like a factory whistle. He had not, in actual fact, chosen this woman for himself. Just as young Crow had exploited 'that Man' to disguise his own weakness, Suguro had married this woman in order to satisfy those around him.

He had been twenty-eight at the time. His mother had died during his fourth year at middle school, and he and Sakiko, having no other recourse, had gone to live with their father.

His father would often say to him, 'I'm going to find you someone to marry. I failed in my marriage, you know. A young man doesn't know how to choose a woman.'

These phlegmatic words and the self-satisfied look on his father's face depressed Suguro. He rebelled at the idea of someone else meddling in his marriage prospects. But he also bristled at the insulting remarks his father had made about his late mother. He remembered the countless evenings at his uncle's home in Mikage, and his mother's tear-stained face as she cursed her husband and complained to her brother-in-law and sister. There was something disagreeable about her weepy face. Still, it belonged to his mother. He felt as though he would be intensifying the solitude in that face if he married someone picked out to suit his father's tastes.

Suguro and his sister seldom mentioned their mother after moving to their father's house. Before long their lives in their new home were such that their mother virtually ceased to exist for them. She was no longer a part of their daily activities, as though the yellowed photographs of her had all been ripped from the pages of their family album. Suguro accommodated himself to that life, feeling all the while unbearably distraught with himself for doing so.

In no time his sister had been married off to a young man of her father's choosing.

'I don't want to have to carry our parents' past around with me for ever,' she said to Suguro one day. 'I have my own life to live.'

A self-seeking logic flowed like an undercurrent beneath her remark, intimating that Suguro needed to start behaving like a man of the twentieth century and throw off the memories of his mother that weighed upon him like a millstone. He did not try to refute her, but he hated her for suggesting it.

She came twice a month to her father's house in the Nakano section of Tokyo. She liked Suguro to see how happy she was with her husband and child.

'Father, it's time we found Shin-chan a wife,' Sakiko's husband remarked. Since he was older than Suguro, he felt free to use the familiar 'Shin-chan'. He was the sort of fellow who would put on his gardening shoes and go out to help his father-in-law trim the bonsai trees without even being asked.

'You're right,' Suguro's father answered as he worked the pruning scissors. 'But he's got so many qualifications for a wife, I don't know what to do.'

'But he couldn't go wrong marrying someone you chose, Father. Isn't that so, Shin-chan?'

From the veranda, where she was dressing their three-year-old child in white woollen trousers, Sakiko chimed in, 'He's right. You've got to choose someone for him.'

That triumphant face, so unlike her mother's. Her nose was pointed and slightly upturned. From childhood it had been her nature to suppress her own feelings, even the deepest feelings of her heart, if that would keep the waves from rising in her life. Now that attitude was directed towards this husband who was watering his father-in-law's bonsai in the garden. Suguro wondered what sort of look she had on her face when she and her husband made love.

He came up with various excuses to reject the photographs of marriage prospects that poured into his father's hands one after another from acquaintances. Only once had he reluctantly attended an *omiai* interview. The woman had performed a tea ceremony for Suguro at a temple in Kamakura.

'What's wrong with you? Don't you want to get married?'

When those negotiations fell apart, Suguro was summoned to his father's room, where the older man was sitting with a sour expression on his face. He heated a tiny teacup in hot water, and while it was still warm, poured some green tea into it. Suguro studied his father's gaunt, slender hands in silence.

'Is there someone else you like?'

'Mmm,' he lied. 'But I don't know how she feels.'

In reality there was no woman he was interested in. He knew five or six, but they were only casual acquaintances.

'If that's the case,' his father picked up the teacup and scowled at the thickly-planted garden, 'why didn't you tell me sooner?'

A month later Suguro proposed to the woman who was now his wife. He felt for her none of the passion a young man has for a woman, and he first brought up the subject of marriage with her at a cheap noodle shop. He had chosen this unromantic setting deliberately, in an effort to remind himself that for him this proposal was purely a business arrangement. He wanted to block out all the matches his father was trying to make for him; he would marry any girl at all, so long as his choice was one that did no damage to the image of the ugly, weeping face of his mother that he kept within his heart. The woman he finally selected had the least charm of any of the five or six women he knew socially. She was as plain as a pear blossom, unobtrusive and reserved. At parties she sat quietly in a corner, looking out at the world with her rice-ball face.

Between sips of his soup at the noodle shop, he brought up the topic of marriage, and the rice-ball face quivered and gaped at him in disbelief.

Even after they were married and living together, Suguro sometimes recalled that look on her face with a certain degree of anguish. His wife had no idea what he had been feeling then. She did not know that he had decided to marry her from the selfish wish not to betray his dead mother. She would probably live out her life never realizing that he had chosen her not because he loved her, but because he was weak.

By degrees his wife had grown fat and ugly. Sometimes that made him lose his temper. Suguro seldom argued with her, but that did not mean they were satisfied with each other. Once, one winter evening as she sat with the baby beside her, he had struck her and blurted out words that should never have been spoken. 'I never really wanted you.'

The rice-ball face stared fixedly at Suguro, and tears slowly coursed down its cheeks.

Still, whether he had really wanted her or not, Suguro at the very least had to admit that he had chosen this particular woman to be his wife. That was evidenced by the fact that she resided with him beneath the same roof, toiled beside him, and was the mother of his child. Satisfied with her or not, she was the woman who shared her life with Suguro. He had convinced himself that his motives for choosing her had not been the pure sort of love that other men felt for their wives, but for him the puffed-up, pretentious word 'love' had the same hollow ring to it as 'faith' or 'baptism'. Gradually 'love' took on a new meaning in Suguro's mind. People were drawn to beautiful things, attractive things. But that feeling was not really love.

'I never really wanted you.'

The night he had slapped her and spoken those words, and seen the tears streaming down her face, Suguro had realized that above all else this woman was his wife. Now, with her weak heart, she gasped as she flung charcoal and firewood into the furnace. Her eyelids and cheeks were swollen, and white ash clung to her hair. Hers was the weary face common to virtually every housewife. But it was, after all, a face of Suguro's own fashioning. It was one of his life-works, like the clumsy stories he produced by gathering and blending his materials and impatiently committing them to paper. And behind her weary face, Suguro discovered yet another face of someone he had not really wanted. He discovered the debilitated face of 'that Man', a person he had cursed and despised and beaten throughout his days.

Just as his wife had accepted his proposal in the noodle shop without knowing what lay in his heart, 'that Man' had come to live with Suguro, believing the perfunctory catechetical oath Crow had unlovingly vowed one winter morning in the church at Shukugawa. Like his wife, 'that Man' had been his companion now for over thirty years, wheezing like a steam whistle, and with the same ugly face.

When Suguro cursed the Man and declared he had never really wanted Him, sad, dog-like eyes peered back at him, and tears slowly trickled down those cheeks. The face was not the imposing visage that the religious artists had painted, but a face that belonged only to Suguro, that only he knew. Just as I will never leave my wife, I will never abandon you. I have tormented you the same way I have tormented my wife. I'm not at all sure that I will not go on abusing you as I do her. But I will never cast you off utterly.

The rain finally stopped. Suguro took his son and walked down the road from the hill and through the puddles to buy some cigarettes at the shop by the station. Clouds were still piled up in the sky like clumps of used cotton, but faint rays of sunlight seeped through the few gaps and shimmered on the surface of the puddles.

'That's a stink-weed. It'll make your hands smell,' Suguro scolded his son, who was crouched in a clump of grass tearing off white flowers. 'Come on, hurry up. Leave those there.'

'Is this the grove?'

'What grove?'

'The one in the story you told me.' The boy hurled a stone into the thicket of trees.

FUDA-NO-TSUJI

Whenever he boarded the streetcar he always recalled a short sketch by Nagai Kafū which he had read in school. It was an essay in which Kafū observed the passengers who got on and off a tottering old train between one station and the terminal, and tried to imagine what sort of life each person led. At present the man led a life in which books played no part, but for some reason he thought of Kafū's piece every time he climbed on a streetcar.

It was an autumn afternoon, and rain was falling. He sat down on the hard seat and began his journey towards the Ginza.

After many years of being out of touch with them, he was setting out for a reunion with the classmates whose desks had surrounded his so long ago. Actually, he was not eager to have his old classmates see him in his rumpled suit and worn shoes. But when one of them phoned him at his office the previous day, he had meekly agreed to attend the gathering.

The streetcar was filled with the smells of musty umbrellas, mud and human bodies. As he glanced around at the middle-school students and the lacklustre businessmen so like himself, without particularly intending to mimic Kafū, he wondered about their lives. Perhaps the middle-aged man across the aisle, wearing a suit with frayed sleeves, was an insurance salesman. Likely he would live in a tiny suburban house, and when he got home from work he would sit across from his wife and chew his dinner with a look of discontentment; then he would lie back without a word and listen to the radio – it was as if this middle-aged fellow's entire daily routine had been set out before his eyes. Off to one side sat a woman with a soiled bandage wound around her throat – thanks to some bronchial disorder, she probably spent each day seated like a docile cow in dark hospital waiting-rooms.

As he mused over these ephemeral life histories, the man naturally came to feel a deep antipathy towards them. 'What wretched lives they lead,' he muttered to himself, but the words rebounded into his face as he sat there in his wrinkled suit, heading for his school reunion.

Through the grimy window he could see the rain-soaked streets of the city. The roads had been dug up and houses had been demolished in preparation for the building of an expressway; it reminded him of how the city had looked during the war. The drab telephone poles were plastered with advertisements for everything from Kibun stew to Sanyo televisions.

To the side of the road a young man in a rubber raincoat was repairing a stalled truck. The man on the streetcar detested the filthy houses, the muddy roads and the rainy sky. He knew of nothing that could form a link between himself and this outer world.

'Fuda-no-Tsuji. Our next stop is Fuda-no-Tsuji.' It was almost sunset when the weary voice of the conductor called out over the shoulders of the passengers. By now only the gasoline stations, the tiny buildings and the tree-covered bluff etched blackly against the sky were reflected in the man's eyes. Beyond the bluff stood a large, white, exclusive condominium. A tiny cemetery nestled below, and he could remember a camphor tree that grew on a rise above the cemetery. He caught only a brief glimpse from the window, but twenty-one years earlier, on a rainy day like today, he had stood on that bluff and walked through that cemetery.

Shivering in the cold that day, he had tracked along the base of the bluff in the company of a foreign monk they had called Mouse. The path was choked with nettles, and Mouse had crawled along it, his meagre body hunched forward. He was a clumsy fellow, the man remembered, and couldn't even hold an umbrella properly. Rain had spattered the tiny, mousy face so faithful to his nickname.

'What a moron . . .' The man was standing to the side of the nettle patch, his body half concealed beneath his umbrella, relieving himself after holding back longer than he would have wished. He stole a glance at the monk. The trousers that covered those spindly legs were streaked with mud, and his fidgety movements were like a rodent's.

'Mr Inoue, where is Kodenma-chō?' The monk had finally scrambled to the top of the bluff, and his voice was carried on the dark, rain-laced wind.

'Over that way,' Inoue had answered with some annoyance. 'Towards Nihonbashi.'

'Come up here, please. Can you see it from here?'

What the hell's he talking about? the man grumbled to himself, but with a look of resentment he started up the narrow path to the crest of the bluff.

Mouse was a foreign monk who had worked at G. University in Yotsuya, where the man was an undergraduate in those days. Unlike the priests who were their superiors, the monks primarily did office work at the university or performed odd jobs for the monastery.

Of course Mouse was not his real name. Rumour had it that he was a German Jew with a name something like Baflosky or Bilofsky, but not one of the students could twist his tongue far enough to pronounce his real name. They had already given him the nickname Mouse when the man slipped into this mission school after failing the entrance exams at any number of other institutions. When Mouse poked his tiny white head out the window of the school office and passed out student identity cards and registration certificates, both his outward appearance and his diffident manner reminded the students of a fearful rodent thrusting its head from a hole in the ground.

Mouse's timorous behaviour seemed to stem from more than just his basic nature. As the war effort mounted in intensity, foreigners in Japan (even Germans, who were allies) were viewed with increasing suspicion. Apparently any pretext was sufficient for the police and the military to issue warnings to the university, which was run by an ecclesiastical order of the foreign Christian church. From time to time the students caught glimpses of military police keeping surveillance over the monastery on campus. A year before the man had entered the university, a much-discussed occurrence known as the Yasukuni Shrine Incident had taken place. All the newspapers had reported the incident, in which some Christian students had refused to make the pilgrimage to the Yasukuni Shintō shrine, a ritual required by the Ministry of Education on each Imperial Rescript Day.

The year following the incident, a lieutenant-colonel recently returned from the front lines in Northern China was assigned as military overseer at G. University.

On wintry mornings when the air was stretched taut as a bowstring, the students often saw this officer strutting his horse along the moat at Yotsuya. Like a country bumpkin newly arrived in the city, the lieutenant-colonel made an exaggerated display of his own importance in front of the many foreign priests at the school. His well-polished riding-boots glimmered a copper colour in the sun, and when he dismounted in front of the university and stiffened his ruddy, moustached face, the students were expected to salute him. When they heard the leathery creak of those boots, students loitering in the hall and puffing on cigarettes outside classes quickly exchanged knowing glances, crushed out their cigarettes, and fled into the classrooms.

The students were not the only ones to be intimidated by the lieutenant-colonel. The squeak of his boots sometimes echoed from the hallway in the middle of lectures, and the foreign priests would lift their faces uncomfortably from their textbooks. One day, as he listened to the sound of those footsteps gradually retreating into the distance, one of the foreigners softly spat out the word '*Paisant!*'

The man could still remember a cloudy morning on one of the monthly Imperial Rescript Days. The students were assembled on the small school field, where as always they were forced to listen to a droning recitation of the Imperial Rescript and observe the hoisting of the Rising Sun.

The faded flag hung limply against the overcast sky. There were shouted cries of 'Salute!' and then 'Dismissed!' But suddenly the lieutenant-colonel restrained the instructors who had begun to disperse and climbed up on the platform. For a long while he glared at the students with piercing eyes. His childish attempt to assert his authority was ludicrous, but no one dared to laugh or to feign nonchalance by whistling.

'You b-b-bastards!' The lieutenant-colonel tended to stammer when he was overwrought. 'You're all d-d-degenerate. And the f-f-foreigners and staff at this university are all corrupted!'

As the officer ranted, the man studied the faces of the instructors standing on either side of the platform. They were all either tense or expressionless. The cotton-grey sky shuddered with a dull roar as an airplane passed in the distance. An eddy of wind swept up scraps of paper from a corner of the field and swirled them around in a cloud of yellow dust. But everyone listened in silence to the officer's outburst.

Some of the students had ingratiated themselves with the lieutenant-colonel. This they accomplished by intentionally disobeying the priests and monks and treating them with disrespect. In such a climate, the face that Mouse inched out of the window at the Student Affairs Office came to look ever more pale and diffident.

Mouse was unusually short in stature, especially in comparison to the towering figures of the other foreigners. His child-like neck and limbs stood out even next to those of the students decimated by the exigencies of the war situation. His face, too, which rather resembled that of the old movie comedian Harold Lloyd, was the object of ridicule and mockery among the simple-minded students. Various tales of Mouse's faint-heartedness and effeminacy circulated through the student body.

One of them concerned an incident about a year previously, when a student had accidentally fallen from a third-storey window. He had been scuffling with some friends and was leaning against the window when the frame popped out. People flocked to where he had fallen on the ground, but he had already lost consciousness, and his face and hands were bathed in blood from cuts caused by the shards of glass. It was only after the injured student had been carried away on a stretcher that several students noticed Mouse leaning against a telephone pole with a sickly look on his face. The sight of blood on the student's lacerated body had apparently caused the monk to faint.

Another story was spread around campus by the son of the school physician. The year before, Mouse had been hospitalized with a severe case of peritonitis. Unwilling to rely on Japanese doctors, he had wept and pleaded with his superior to summon a foreign doctor for him.

Feverish and perspiring profusely, Mouse had lost all sense of shame, and to every nurse and visitor who came to see him had wailed, 'I don't want to die! I'm afraid to die!' By his pillow he had placed photographs of his mother and younger sister. The room was permeated with the stifling cheesy smell of a foreigner. But the students got their biggest laugh when the doctor's son announced that he had got a glimpse of Mouse's sexual organ.

'His thing's as tiny as a string-bean!' was the report.

Having smelled the cheesy odour, heard the infantile moans of a man afraid of death, and seen (at least vicariously) that the monk's penis was no larger than a bean, the students' laughter soon turned to scorn. At a time when their country was at war with the Caucasian, they were stirred occasionally by a desire to torment Mouse in some sadistic fashion.

It was in the midst of such an atmosphere that Mouse and the man were brought together one evening.

For no special reason the man had remained at school after classes until late that evening. Sitting with his chin in his hands in the middle of a dusty, deserted classroom, he was staring vacantly out at the crimson sky, the darkening waters of the moat and the coal-black houses.

As he sat there absent-mindedly, from the far end of the hall came the squeak of riding-boots. Initially the sound did not register in his head, coming as it did that late in the evening, but when he became fully conscious of it he instinctively bolted from the classroom into the hallway.

'H-h-halt! Aren't you going to salute me?'

The man stood awkwardly at attention while the officer asked his name and ordered him to repeat the Imperial Rescript graciously bequeathed to the Japanese people by their military rulers.

The man faltered for words. He had forgotten that during military exercises the students had been ordered to be prepared to recite the rescript at any time. In an attempt to mask his embarrassment, he managed to produce a faint smile. But the tactic was ill-conceived.

'Impudence!' The officer struck him across the face with his fist. When he tried to shield his face with his left arm, that arm received the second blow. Doubtless the man would have been beaten some more if Mouse had not suddenly blundered onto the scene.

Mouse had not come to rescue him. By mere chance he had opened the door of the office at the end of the hall and ventured a look with his Harold Lloyd face. Motionless, and with terrified eyes, the monk gazed at the thread of blood curling down the man's cheek, and at the dark red face of the officer.

Under different circumstances, the lieutenant-colonel might have walked away at this point; instead he encountered the startled gaze of the monk. The fact that the gawking figure belonged to a Caucasian triggered an explosion of the peculiar complex Japanese feel in the presence of foreigners. Shouting two or three words the monk could not understand, he grabbed hold of Mouse's habit and jerked him out into the hallway.

'Your ap-p-proach to education at this school is totally misguided!'

Once the lieutenant-colonel had stomped away, the man wiped the blood from his mouth with the palm of his hand, then began spitting blood out of the window. When he had finished, he turned around. In a corner of the dark hallway, Mouse stood as though frozen. His eyes lowered, the man skulked away.

Even in such an atmosphere, some of the foreign priests and staff workers quietly did what they could to preserve the traditional climate of the university. For instance, monthly gatherings of the 'Christian Research Association' were convened in a tiny reading-room of the library by students in the history department. These were, perhaps, a subtle form of protest against the trend of the times.

Although he didn't have the slightest interest in Christianity, the man once looked in on one of their meetings, solely out of a desire to escape from the increasing oppressiveness of student life and the mounting bloodthirstiness of the world outside.

He walked in just as a young Japanese history teacher was describing some of the landmarks of the Christian period in Tokyo. The man stood listlessly behind a group of thirty or so students. Needless to say, the discussion failed to arouse his interest. Instead he felt out of place, regretting that he had come as he glanced around at the diligent students avidly taking notes and at the backs of the solemn, white-haired, foreign missionaries.

He found the discussion hard to follow, but it seemed to be about fifty martyrs executed at Fuda-no-Tsuji at the time of the Shōgun Iemitsu.

In the tenth month of 1623 the authorities, receiving a report from an informer, arrested the leading Christians who were in hiding in Edo and placed them in a prison at Kodenma-chō. Two months later these prisoners, together with two foreign priests, were taken along the road past Muromachi, Kyōbashi, Hamamatsu-chō and Mita, to the execution ground at Fuda-no-Tsuji, where they were lashed to fifty stakes and burned to death.

Even now the man could remember bits and pieces of the discussion. One portion he particularly recalled concerned the conditions in the prisons at that time, which the young instructor described with quotations from the correspondence of Friar San Francisco, who had personally witnessed the situation.

The prison at Kodenma-chō was partitioned into four cells. The ceilings were low, and a single hole, barely large enough to accommodate a tiny plate of food, was the only meagre source of light. The Christians were placed in front of these cells, stripped of all their clothing and possessions down to their loincloths, deprived even of their priceless rosaries, and then forced into the cells by a shove from the guards.

Prisoners crouched virtually on top of one another in the dark, cramped cells. When the Christians were thrust inside, they jostled against the scraggy bodies and bony limbs of the other prisoners. At the same instant, their noses were assailed by a loathsome stench.

Each cell was only ten metres deep and four metres wide, and the prisoners were made to sit in three rows. Those in the first and third rows faced one another, while those in the second row huddled between them. They were packed in like sardines, and it was impossible for any of them to get into a standing position. Neither could they extend their arms or legs. Lice and fleas roamed at will over the nearly naked bodies.

Since they could not move, the prisoners, including those who were diseased, urinated and defecated where they sat. This was the source of the foul odour that startled the new arrivals when they entered the cells. Once a day food was inserted through the tiny holes provided, but it was snatched away and gobbled up by those still sound of body. A paltry amount of water was portioned out twice daily, but due to the unbearably sweltering heat inside the cells and the press of bodies, the prisoners ceaselessly flapped their cracked tongues in quest of water.

Besides the guard who stood watch outside the cells, twenty-four officers constantly patrolled the grounds, calling out to each other in loud voices. Whenever the prisoners grew restless in their cells, these officers would climb up and relieve themselves on top of the prisoners. As a result, the bodies of the captives were covered with filth, to the point that they were indistinguishable from one another. Invariably at least one prisoner died each day. Sometimes the corpses were left untouched for seven or eight days. Before long the smell of the decomposing bodies blended with the stench of excrement to torment the Christians.

As the young teacher quoted San Francisco's letter describing the conditions at the Kodenma-chō prison, a sound somewhere between a sigh and a gasp filled the darkening room, and shudders wracked the body of each listener. The war situation was gradually intensifying; the streets were blackened and food shortages were becoming a daily phenomenon. But life in wartime Tokyo still seemed vastly superior to that in the Edo period.

Like the other students, the man listened to the account of these brutal scenes as though he were watching an old silent movie. Such events seemed to belong to a long-departed age that had nothing to do with their own lives.

Among the incarcerated Christians were two Spanish friars and a warrior named Hara Mondo. A son of the Hara clan in Chiba and a close retainer of Shōgun Iemitsu, Mondo turned a deaf ear to the entreaties and admonitions of those around him and clung to his Christian faith. It is reported that after his second arrest the tendons of his arms and legs were severed, and before he was taken to Kodenma-chō the mark of the cross was branded into his face.

As he listened to the tales of martyrdom, the man felt as though he were standing in a rainstorm gazing far into the distance at a sunlit hill. It wasn't merely that these were men and women of faith who had lived in the distant past. They must have been endowed with a strength of will and an innate fortitude utterly unknown to one like himself who had no faith in spiritual things. Or perhaps what impelled them was a kind of fanaticism. For some reason, as the instructor described the manner of their deaths, the man painfully recalled his own miserable beating by the lieutenant-colonel several nights before. He had vivid, remorseful memories of himself trying to flee away with his arm covering his face.

Just before the meeting concluded, the man caught sight of Mouse sitting beside some students in a corner of the dark reading-room. Mouse had also been humiliated, been dragged out by his robes into the hallway. For the monk to be sitting blithely at this meeting struck him as somehow typical of Mouse – laughable and perhaps smacking of hypocrisy. He superimposed this image of hypocrisy over the stories he had heard of the nauseating smell of cheese Mouse had emitted in the hospital, and the anecdote about his bean-like sex organ.

When the gathering broke up, the man smothered a yawn and set off down the stairs alongside the musty-smelling students who had been at the meeting. Mouse caught up with him and started walking beside him, his eyes squinting behind his glasses.

'Excuse me, but can you tell me where Fuda-no-Tsuji is?'

'Fuda-no-Tsuji?'

'They were just talking about it in there.'

The man remembered vaguely that Fuda-no-Tsuji was the place where the fifty Christians had been killed. It annoyed him that Mouse had picked on him instead of one of the other students. *Maybe this fool thinks we're kindred spirits because we were victimized together the other night. Or perhaps he's trying to justify his own cowardice by talking to me.* At this thought, the man stopped on the stairs and peered into Mouse's face.

'Yeah. I know where Fuda-no-Tsuji is, but –'

'Would you take me there? To Fuda-no-Tsuji?'

'Well . . .' Trapped, the man fumbled for words.

Still, one rainy evening the two set out for Fuda-no-Tsuji. They got off the bus and walked a short distance in the direction of Shinagawa. Standing between a tobacconist's and a greengrocer's was a small temple called Chifukuji. Mouse had learned from the young historian that this temple was on the site of the former execution ground.

A tiny cemetery took up most of the temple plot; its edge was walled off by a black bluff covered with nettles. On the slope, amidst a tangled maze of arrowroot, two hemp palms and an old camphor tree spread their branches. Further up was a lush grove of oak and nettle-trees that seemed to be the sole remnants of those early days.

In the drizzle, the man and Mouse stood on the bluff beneath umbrellas. The sky and the houses and roads below them were disappearing in a rainy evening haze sullied by smoke from a factory near the ocean at Shinagawa.

'Then Kodenma-chō is over that way?'

'I think so.' It was of course impossible to see Kodenma-chō clearly in all that mist, so the man gave an irritated, noncommittal answer.

The Christians, carrying on their shoulders placards inscribed with their names, were paraded around on foot from Kodenma-chō to Shimbashi and Mita. The names on the placards were common in Edo – Kakuzaemon, Yosaku, Kudayū, Shinshichirō, Kisaburō. At the rear of the procession, Hara Mondo rode on the back of a saddleless horse.

At the execution ground, faggots of firewood were stacked at the base of the fifty stakes. A mob of spectators had already assembled outside, nibbling at their lunches and sipping hot tea as they waited for the hour of the execution. Suddenly one of the fifty prisoners, catching sight of the execution ground, began to shout that he would abandon his faith. His ropes were loosened and he was released on the spot.

When the Christians had been lashed to the stakes, the guards walked around setting fire to the wood. It was a windy day, so the flames and smoke quickly engulfed the stakes and their captives. The two Spanish priests were the first to expire, followed by Hara Mondo, who drew his arms together as though cradling something within them before his head dropped to his shoulder.

As he stood at the place that had once been an execution ground, the man realized that those scenes which had seemed part of an old movie had been enacted beneath his very feet. His eyes began to swim. Yet he could not rid himself of the feeling that the martyrs were far removed from his own life. Only those, like them, who were strong and specially appointed could carry out such superhuman acts. They lived on a higher plane that the one where he subsisted.

At this thought, he stole a quick glance at the rain-drenched monk beside him. The man could almost imagine what thoughts were passing through Mouse's head. For himself, a simple student who made no claims to religious belief, these martyrs were no more than abstract images of people from a far distant world. But however true to his nickname he might be, Mouse here was an ascetic who had come to Japan to pursue a religious vocation. So it must be with unbearable shame that he compared his own cowardly disposition with the determination of these Japanese martyrs.

You couldn't do what they did. I might be worthless myself, but there's no way you could do it, either.

Being the kind of person he was, the man could surmise the limitations of someone like Mouse. Once a coward, always a coward; he could never attain the firm resolve of Hara Mondo and the other martyrs. Mouse and the man had both been abused by the lieutenant-colonel in that hallway, and both had lacked the courage even to run away. In both of them, the spirit was powerless in the face of bodily danger. He and Mouse belonged to the group that would have done anything to apostatize before reaching the execution ground.

'Do you have any family back in your country?' he asked, stirred for the first time with curiosity about Mouse. The monk's body jerked, as though he had been awakened from a dream.

'What?'

'Do you have a family in Germany?'

'Yes. My mother and a younger sister live in Köln.'

'Why did you become a monk?'

Mouse clutched his umbrella and did not reply. The rain had finally let up, but the area was swathed in thick darkness. The man set out first down the hill, planting his feet wide apart to keep from slipping down the wet incline.

Thereafter he seldom even spoke to Mouse at school. The war continued to rage, and before long the air raids commenced. In place of classes, the students were transported each day to do work at a factory in Kawasaki. The Yotsuya area around the campus was burned by fire bombs, and at some point the man realized that Mouse had disappeared from the school office. Someone said he had been sent back to Germany, but by then the man had forgotten that they had even climbed that hill together.

As the streetcar passed Fuda-no-Tsuji, the man momentarily recalled that day twenty-one years earlier. He remembered, but he felt no particular emotion.

When he got off the streetcar at Shimbashi, the neon lights were glistening in the rain, and buses and taxis were splashing up mud as they sped by. The reunion was being held at a restaurant called 'Fūgetsu'. No sooner had he arrived than he wished he had not come. His wrinkled suit was soaked from the rain, making him look even more bedraggled, while his old classmates all seemed to have arrived in taxis, their hair neatly parted, white handkerchiefs peeking out of their breast pockets. There were some who clapped him on the shoulder nostalgically, but these sporadic gestures only depressed him, making him feel as though he was an object of sympathy.

He sat down at one corner of the long, narrow dinner-table, wishing he had stayed home as he silently sipped his black tea. Once the group at the table had reported on their present jobs and situations and swapped name-cards, the conversation turned to rumours about those absent and recollections of their teachers. With vaguely envious eyes the man watched as counterfeit friendships were struck up all around him.

'What's happened to Sayama?'

'Oh, he's living in Mie Prefecture. He works in the shipping industry.'

'There was a teacher named Roku, wasn't there?'

'Yes, yes. He's still teaching.'

How odd at a time like this that they should all pretend to have loved their alma mater, the man thought peevishly. He had no affection for his school and did not feel the least bit nostalgic about his classmates.

'Whatever became of Mouse? You remember him – he worked in the office.'

For the first time the man lifted his face from his teacup and listened attentively. But it seemed that many of the group could not even remember the name Mouse. With a chuckle someone reminded the group of the looks and mannerisms of the cowardly monk, and finally there were exclamations of 'Oh, him!'

Then a man named Mukai, who had stayed at the school and become a teacher there, chimed in: 'I heard a peculiar story about him.' After Mouse's return to Germany, he had been arrested because he was a Jew and put into a concentration camp. It was a camp set up in a village called Dachau, near the Polish border. There had been no further word about him.

'But a little while back, Bita told me about an article he'd read in a foreign newspaper.'

Bita was a foreign priest who taught Law at the university. He had read in a newspaper from his homeland about a monk in the Dachau camp who had died in the place of one of his comrades. When one of the Jews in the camp was sentenced to death by starvation, the monk had offered himself as a subtitute and died as a result.

'It said the monk had once done missionary work in Japan.'

'Do you think it was Mouse?'

'I don't know. Apparently his name didn't appear in the article. But Bita said –'

'How could it have been Mouse? With the kind of temperament he had . . . ? And besides, he didn't come to Japan to do missionary work, did he?'

Recollections of the time Mouse nearly fainted at the sight of blood, and the legend about his bean-sized penis briefly poured out from the group amid much laughter. That Harold Lloyd face peering out from the dark office to pass out student cards and discount passes. The mousy figure scurrying around the campus, flashing feeble smiles. The well-groomed, neatly-attired graduates finally sang their school song and the party broke up.

After the reunion they all flagged down individual taxis and headed for a Ginza bar for a second round. The man walked alone through the rain to the streetcar stop. As before, the streetcar was steeped in the smells of wet umbrellas, mud and human bodies. Glancing around at the passengers, who seemed as commonplace as he, the man again mimicked Kafū and tried to imagine what sorts of lives these people led. The young man across the way pulled out a pencil and, spreading out a bicycle-racing form, began to write something down. A girl who looked as though she was on her way home from evening classes was dozing with a Crown Reader on her lap. All these passengers, like the man himself, surely led faded lives of cowardice and would be buried cowards. Yet, when the streetcar passed Fuda-no-Tsuji, the man wiped the mist from the window with his fingers and peered intently out.

The bluff towered blackly behind the faintly-lit shops and houses. He did not know what kind of place Dachau was. But years before he had seen newsreel photos of a concentration camp. It had seemed much like the Kodenma-chō prison where the Christians had been incarcerated. The realization that Mouse had been in such a place filled the man with wonderment. And if, in fact, Mouse had died for a friend – for love – then that was not a tale from the long-gone days of the Edo period, but an incident that commanded a place in the man's own heart. Who or what had effected such a change in Mouse? Who or what had carried Mouse to such a distant point? The man shook his head and looked across at the sleeping girl and the young man hunched over his gambling sheets. Somewhere in this crowd – yes, somewhere in this crowd, he thought, sitting with his Harold Lloyd face, his mud-splattered knees quivering, was Mouse.

THE DAY BEFORE

For some time I had wanted to get my hands on that *fumie*. If nothing else, I at least wanted to be able to see it. The image was owned by Tokujirō Fukae of Daimyō village, Sonoki, in Nagasaki Prefecture. A copper engraving of the crucified Christ was set in a wooden frame eight inches wide by twelve inches in length.

It had been used during the fourth siege of Urakami, the final persecution of Christians in Japan. Use of the *fumie* was supposed to have been abolished by the US-Japan Treaty of 1858, but apparently it was used again in this suppression, which occurred after the signing of the accord.

My desire to obtain the *fumie* was aroused when I read in a Catholic tract about Tōgorō, a villager from Takashima in Sonoki District, who apostatized during the fourth siege. The tract fascinated me. Its author of course confined himself to presenting the historical facts surrounding the suppression and said very little about Tōgorō, but my interest was riveted on him.

Father N., a friend from my school-days, happened to be in Nagasaki at the time, so I wrote to him about my feelings concerning Tōgorō. In his reply he mentioned the *fumie*. Daimyō village was in his parish, he noted, and a Mr Fukae from the village owned a *fumie* from the period. It seems that some of Mr Fukae's ancestors had been among the officials who had carried out the suppression.

The day before I was due to have my third operation, arrangements were made for me to see the *fumie*. My friend Father Inoue was supposed to go to Nagasaki and bring it back with him. This was not merely for my benefit, of course; his assignment was to deposit the image in the Christian Archives at J. University in Yotsuya. That was a disappointment to me, but I conceded the necessity of preserving such precious objects. Father Inoue telephoned my wife and let her know he would be allowed to give me a brief look at it before he turned it over to the archives.

I dozed off in my hospital room as I waited for Father Inoue.

Christmas was approaching, and I could hear a choir practising on the roof – probably students from the school of nursing. Sometimes I would open my eyes a slit and listen to those voices in the distance, then close my eyes again.

I sensed someone softly opening the door to my room. It might be my wife, I thought, but she was supposed to be running around making all the arrangements for my massive surgery tomorrow. So I couldn't imagine it would be her.

'Who's there?'

A middle-aged man dressed in a fur jacket and a mountaineering cap peered in. I did not know him. I glanced first from his dirty cap to his fur jacket, then lowered my gaze to the large lace-up boots he was wearing. Ah, this is someone from Father Inoue, I thought.

'Are you from the church?'

'Huh?'

'Father sent you, didn't he?' I smiled, but his eyes narrowed and a strange expression crossed his face.

'No. I asked 'em over in the ward, and they said you might wanna buy.'

'Buy? What?'

'You get four for six hundred yen. I got books, too. But I didn't bring 'em today.'

Not waiting for me to respond, he appeared to twist at the waist and pulled a small paper envelope from his trouser pocket. Inside the envelope were four photographs with yellowed borders, a result no doubt of cheap developing. In the shadowy prints the dim figure of a man embraced the indistinct body of a woman. A single wooden chair stood beside the bed in what appeared to be a dreary hotel in the suburbs.

'You don't understand. I'm being operated on tomorrow!'

'That's why I brought these.' He had no words of sympathy to offer. Scratching the palm of his hand with the photographs, he continued, 'Since you got an operation coming up, you can buy these as a good-luck charm. Buy 'em and the operation's bound to be a success. How about it, captain?'

'Do you come around to this hospital often?'

'Sure. This is my territory.'

It may have been a joke, or perhaps he meant it seriously, but he made the declaration to me with all the bravura of a physician talking to one of his patients. I took a liking to the man.

'No, no. These pictures don't interest me.'

'Well . . .' He looked rueful. 'If you don't like these, what sort of pose do you want, captain?'

He lit up a cigarette from the pack I held out to him and began to chatter.

Nowhere does a person get more bored and develop a greater desire to look at pictures and books of this sort than in hospital. No location was more suitable to peddle such goods, since the police would never suspect. This fellow had divided up the territory with his colleagues and made the rounds of the city hospitals.

'A few days back, the old boy in Room H took a look at these shots before his operation, and he says, "Ah, now I can die happy!"'

I laughed. This pedlar was a more welcome visitor today than the relatives who tiptoe through hospital-room doors with pained looks on their faces. When he had finished his cigarette, he stuck another behind his ear and left my room.

For some reason I felt in high spirits. This pedlar had come instead of Father. Bringing pornographic pictures in place of the *fumie*. Today should have been a day for me to think about many things, to put various affairs in order. Tomorrow's operation would be unlike my first two; the doctors anticipated massive haemorrhaging and danger because my pleurae had fused together. The risk was so great they had left it up to me whether or not to go through with surgery. Today I had intended to put on a face so bland it would seem that cellophane had been stretched over it, but that porn pedlar had nipped that plan in the bud. But, after all, those murky photographs with their sallow images were proof of God's existence.

When the officers of the feudal domain raided Takashima, the villagers were reciting their evening prayers. They naturally had look-outs posted, but the police were already storming into the farmhouse chapel when the sentries rang the warning bell.

In the light of the moon that night, ten men – including two leaders of the peasant association – were hurriedly transported to Urakami. Among them, for good or ill, was Tōgorō. From the outset his comrades had the uneasy foreboding that Tōgorō would apostatize. He had been such an irksome anomaly in this village of fervent faith. Despite his massive stature, Tōgorō was a coward.

On past occasions Tōgorō had been lured into quarrels by the young men of neighbouring villages. Though he was twice the size of an average man, there were times when he skulked back to Takashima clad only in his loin-cloth, having been thrown to the ground and stripped of all he had. Fear of his opponents rather than a Christian conviction to turn the other cheek prevented him from offering any resistance at such times. It was not long before the villagers of Takashima came to despise him. For that reason, although he was already thirty years old, he was the only young man of his age without a bride. He lived alone with his mother.

Of the ten prisoners, Kashichi held the highest position in the village. He was a man of principle, and the evening before the interrogations began at Urakami, he offered special words of encouragement to Tōgorō. 'Deus and Santa Maria will surely grant us strength and courage. Those who suffer in this world will certainly be resurrected in heaven,' Kashichi reassured him. Tōgorō studied the others with the terrified eyes of a stray dog, but at their urging he joined in the chanting of the Credo and the Our Father.

Early in the morning on the following day, the interrogations began at the office of the Urakami magistrate. The prisoners were bound and dragged out one by one to the cold, gravel-floored interrogation room, where the officers brought out the *fumie*. Those who would not recant their faith were beaten severely with an archer's bow. But before the bow had even been raised over Tōgorō, he ground his soiled foot into the face of Christ in the image. With sad, animal-like eyes Tōgorō darted a glance towards his comrades, who were dishevelled and covered with blood. The officers then drove him out of the magistrate's headquarters.

'We're going to shave you and get a blood sample now.' This time a nurse came into my room, carrying a metal tray and a hypodermic. Her job was to shave the fine hairs from the area targeted for surgery tomorrow and to determine my blood type for transfusions.

When she removed my pyjama top the chilly air cut into my skin. I raised my left arm and did my best not to giggle as she moved the razor along my armpit.

'That tickles!'

'When you bathe, be sure to wash really well back here. It's all red.'

'I can't wash there. It's been very sensitive since my last operation. I can't scrub it.'

There is a large scar on my back, cut at a slant across my shoulder. The area is swollen, since an incision was made twice in the same place. Again tomorrow the cold scalpel will race across that spot. And my body will be soaked with blood.

After Tōgorō's desertion the remaining nine men stubbornly refused to apostatize. They were placed for a time in a Nagasaki prison, and the following year – 1868 – they were loaded into a boat and sent to Tsuyama, near Onomichi. Rain fell that evening and drenched the open boat, and the prisoners, having only the clothes they were wearing, huddled together to ward off the cold. As the boat pulled away from Nagasaki, one of the prisoners, Bunji, noticed a man dressed like a dockworker standing at the edge of the water.

'Look! Isn't that Tōgorō?'

From far in the distance, Tōgorō was peering towards them with the same sad, appealing eyes they had seen when he apostatized. The men lowered their eyes as though they had gazed upon something filthy, and no one uttered another word.

The prison for these nine men lay in the mountains some twenty-four miles from Tsuyama. From their cell they could see the officers' hut and a small pond. At first there was little harassment, and the officers were lenient. Even the food they received twice a day was something for which these impoverished farmers could be thankful. The officers laughed gently and told them that they could eat better food and be given warmer clothes if they would merely cast off their burdensome religion.

In the autumn of that year, fourteen or fifteen new prisoners arrived unexpectedly. They were children from Takashima. The men were surprised at this strange move by the officials, yet pleased to be able to see some of their relatives after so long a time. But soon they were forced into the realization that this move was part of a psychological torture they came to refer to as 'child abuse.'

Occasionally the prisoners heard weeping from the adjoining cell, where their children were incarcerated. One afternoon a prisoner named Fujifusa pressed his face to the tiny window of the children's cell and saw two emaciated boys catching dragonflies and stuffing them into their mouths. It was obvious that the children were being given scarcely anything that could be called food. The other men listened to this report and wept.

They begged the officers to take even half of their own 'fine' food and share it with the children, but this was not allowed. They were told, however, that all they needed do was reject their troublesome religion, and they and their children would go back to their dear village pleasingly plump.

'There. All done.'

The nurse pulled out the hypodermic, and as I rubbed the spot where the needle had entered, she held the vial filled with blood up to the light at eye level.

'Your blood is dark, isn't it?'

'Does it mean something's wrong if it's dark?'

'Oh, no. I was just commenting on how dark it is.'

As she went out, a young doctor I had not seen before came in. I tried to sit up in bed.

'No, no. As you were. I'm Okuyama of Anaesthesia.'

Okuyama turned out to be the anaesthetist who would assist at my operation the next day. He went through the formality of placing a stethoscope on my chest.

'In your previous operations, did you awaken quickly from the anaesthesia?'

In my most recent operation, the doctors had cut away five of my ribs. I remembered that the anaesthesia had worn off just as the operation ended. The pain I experienced then was like a pair of scissors jabbing through my chest. I described the agony for Okuyama.

'This time, please keep me knocked out for at least half a day. That was terribly painful.'

The young doctor smiled broadly. 'We'll aim for that, then.'

When it became clear that the men were still not going to apostatize, the tortures began. The nine men were separated and placed in small boxes, in which they were unable to move from a seated position. Holes were bored near their heads to allow them to breathe. They were not permitted to leave the boxes except to relieve themselves.

Winter drew near. The prisoners began to weaken from cold and exhaustion. In compensation, however, they began to hear laughter from the adjoining cell. The officers, being fathers themselves, had given food to the children. The nine men in their individual boxes listened silently to the laughing voices.

At the end of the eleventh month a prisoner named Kumekichi died. The oldest of the nine, he had been unable to endure the cold and the fatigue. Kashichi had had great respect for the old man and always asked his advice whenever something happened in the prison. He was therefore deeply affected by his death. Peering out through the hole bored in his box, Kashichi reflected on how weak his own will had become. And for the first time he hated the traitor Tōgorō.

Again the door opened softly. Father? No. Once again it was the porn pedlar.

'Captain!'

'What? You!'

'Actually . . . I've brought you a good-luck charm . . .'

'I told you I wouldn't buy any.'

'Not pictures. I'm giving you this for free. Then if your operation's a success, you can thank me by purchasing the pictures and books I bring around.' He lowered his voice to a whisper. 'Captain, I can get you a woman. It's strictly "no trespassing" around here. You can lock the door. You've got a bed. Nobody'll know!'

'Yes, yes.'

He was clutching an object in his hand. Before he left he set it on the table beside my bed. I glanced over and discovered a tiny wooden doll, grimy from the sweat and soil of the pedlar's hands.

They were taken from their boxes when winter came, but the mornings and nights continued cold. From the mountain to the rear they heard sounds like something splitting open. It was the sound of tree branches cracking from the cold. Thin ice stretched across the tiny pond between the prison and the officers' hut.

One day near evening, the officers came and took two prisoners, Seiichi and Tatsugorō, from the cell. They cast the two into the frozen pond and beat them with poles each time their heads bobbed above the surface of the water. When they lost consciousness from the painful torture, Seiichi and Tatsugorō were carried back to the prison in the arms of the officers. The six remaining men joined their voices with Kashichi's and recited the Ave Maria over and over again. But many were choked with sobs during the final benediction, 'Blessed Mary, Mother of God, intercede for us now and in the moment of death.'

Just then, through the cell window Kashichi caught sight of a tall, thin man glancing about him restlessly like a beggar. The man, whose hair and beard grew wantonly like an exile's, turned towards him, and Kashichi involuntarily shouted, 'It's Tōgorō!'

An officer came out to drive the intruder away, but Tōgorō shook his head and seemed to be making some sort of fervent plea. Eventually the first officer summoned another, and the two spoke together for a few moments. Finally they took Tōgorō to the only empty cell in the prison.

'He's one of you,' the officers announced, confusion written on their faces. When they were gone, the eight prisoners sat wordlessly and listened to the sounds of Tōgorō shuffling about in the dark.

'Why did you come?' At last Kashichi asked the question in all their minds. He felt vaguely uneasy. It had occurred to him that Tōgorō might be a spy for the officers. Even if he were not a spy, his presence might further dampen the already weakened spirits of the others. Kashichi had heard from the dead Kumekichi that the officers employed such cunning devices.

Tōgorō's reply was unexpected. In a soft voice, he told them that he had come here and surrendered on his own.

'You . . . ?!'

When the men jeered at him, Tōgorō tried to stammer out a defence. Kashichi silenced them.

'Do you realize that you will be tortured here? If you're going to make it harder for the rest of us, you'd better go back home.'

Tōgorō remained silent.

'Aren't you afraid?'

'I'm afraid,' Tōgorō muttered.

Then he blurted out something very strange. He had come here because he had heard a voice. He had most certainly heard a voice. It had instructed him to go just once more to be with the others. 'Go to them in Tsuyama. And if you fear the tortures, you can run away again. Go to Tsuyama,' the tearful, pleading voice had said.

That night the only noise that broke the stillness outside was the sound of branches splitting on the mountain. The prisoners listened intently to Tōgorō's story. One grumbled, 'A nice convenient tale for him to tell, isn't it?' To him, the story sounded like something Tōgorō had made up so that his friends and fellow villagers would forgive him for his betrayal two years earlier. 'If you fear the tortures, you can run away again.' It seemed just another handy way of talking himself out of difficulty.

Kashichi was half inclined to agree, but another part of him refused to believe that Tōgorō's story was a hoax. Unable to sleep that night, he listened thoughtfully to the rustlings of Tōgorō's body in the darkness.

The following day Tōgorō was taken out by the officers and hurled into the pond. The other prisoners joined Kashichi in reciting the Credo as Tōgorō's childlike screams filled their ears. They prayed that God would grant strength to this weakling. But in the end the voice they heard nullified their entreaties. Tōgorō renounced his faith to the officers and was pulled from the pond.

Still, Kashichi was relieved to know that his suspicions about Tōgorō being a spy had been mistaken. 'It's all right. It's all right,' he thought.

No one knows what happened to Tōgorō after the officers set him free. In 1871, the eight prisoners were released by the new government.

Father Inoue arrived. He opened the door softly and came in, just as the porn pedlar had done. Though it was cold outside, a thin layer of perspiration coated his pale face. We had been friends in our schooldays, and together we had gone to France, sleeping in the hold of a cargo ship among coolies and soldiers.

'I owe you an apology.'

'You couldn't get the *fumie?*'

'No.' Someone higher up in the church hierarchy had ordered another priest to take the *fumie* from Nagasaki to the Christian Archives at J. University.

Inoue had a deep red birthmark on his forehead. He was deacon in a small church in downtown Tokyo. The overcoat he wore had frayed sleeves and his black trousers were worn out at the knees. Just as I had imagined, his figure somehow resembled that of the man in the mountaineering cap. But I told him nothing of that encounter.

Inoue told me that he had seen the *fumie*. The wooden frame was rotting away. The copperplate figure of Christ, covered with greenish rust, had probably been fashioned by a country labourer in Urakami. The face resembled a child's scribble, and the eyes and nose had been worn away until they were no longer distinguishable. The *fumie* had been lying neglected in a storehouse at Mr Fukae's home in Daimyō.

Puffing on our cigarettes, we changed the topic of discussion. I asked Father Inoue about the Last Supper scene in the Gospel of St John. This was a passage that had troubled me for some time. I could not understand the remark Christ made when he handed the sop to the traitor Judas.

'And when he had dipped the sop, he gave it to Judas Iscariot, the son of Simon ... Then said Jesus unto him "That thou doest, do quickly ..."'

That thou doest, do quickly. Obviously referring to Judas' betrayal of Him. But why didn't Christ restrain Judas? Had Jesus really cast the traitor off with such obvious callousness? That was what I wanted to know.

Father Inoue said that these words revealed the human side of Christ. He loved Judas, but with a traitor seated at the same table, He could not suppress His hatred. Father believed that such feeling resembled the complex mixture of love and hate a man feels when he is betrayed by the woman he loves. But I disagreed.

'Jesus isn't issuing a command here. Maybe the translation from the original has been gradually corrupted. It's like He's saying, 'You're going to do this anyway. I can't stop you, so go ahead and do it.' Isn't that what He meant when He said, 'My cross is for that purpose' and spoke of the cross He had to bear? Christ knew all the desperate acts of men.'

The choir practice on the roof seemed to have ended. Afternoons at the hospital were quiet. Sticking with my rather heretical views in spite of Father Inoue's objections, I thought about the *fumie* I had not seen. I had wanted to see it before my operation, but if I couldn't, there was nothing I could do. Father Inoue had reported that the copperplate image of Christ, set in a rotting wooden frame, had been worn away. The feet of the men who had trampled on it had disfigured and gradually rubbed out the face of Christ. But more than that copper image of Christ was disfigured. I think I understand the sort of pain Tōgorō felt in his foot as he trod on it. The pain of many such men was transmitted to the copperplate Christ. And He, unable to endure the sufferings of men, was overwhelmed with compassion and whispered, 'That thou doest, do quickly.' He whose face was trodden upon and he who trod upon it were still alive today, in the same juxtaposition.

Still vaguely in my mind were thoughts of the small, yellow-edged photographs the pedlar had brought in earlier. Just as the shadowy bodies of the man and woman moaned and embraced in those pictures, the face of the copperplate Christ and the flesh of men come into contact with one another. The two strangely resemble one another. This relationship is described in the book of catechisms that children study on Sunday afternoons with nuns in the rear gardens of churches that smell of boiling jam. For many years I scoffed at those catechisms. And yet, after some thirty years, this is the only thing I can say I have learned.

After Father left, I snuggled down into my bed and waited for my wife to come. Occasionally the feeble sunlight shone into my room from between the grey clouds. Steam rose from a medicinal jar on an electric heater. There was a bump as something fell to the floor. I opened my eyes and looked down. It was the good-luck charm the pedlar had given me. That tiny wooden doll, as grimy as life itself.

INCREDIBLE VOYAGE

Late autumn in the year 2005. Yamazato Bontarō, a young physician at the K. University Medical Centre, had just finished making the rounds of the patients' rooms with Dr Yagyū. When he returned to the deserted laboratory, the head nurse came in to tell him that there was a telephone call for him, from a woman.

Conscious of the nurse's ears pricked to hear what he had to say, Bontarō picked up the receiver and said, 'Hello.' He was surprised to hear the voice of Sonomura Sayuri.

'I'm sorry to bother you. I'm just outside the hospital. Do you think you could see me?'

'What's the problem?'

'When I was in class today, I coughed suddenly, and some blood came out.' Sayuri sounded frightened.

'You coughed up blood? Are you sure?'

'Yes. I was frightened and left class early. I came this far, only to find out my brother isn't there.'

Sayuri was a student in the Literature Department at K. University. Her brother Gōichi worked with Bontarō under Dr Yagyū's supervision. The two young men had got to know each another during their first year in medical school; somehow one strong- and one weakwilled fellow had hit it off smoothly, and they had become fast friends.

'Please stay where you are. I'll be right there.'

Bontarō quickly hung up the receiver and left the nurses' station. The prospect of seeing Sayuri made his heart flutter. During his first year at medical school, she had seemed no more than a budding high-school girl, but recently when he dropped in at Gōichi's house, she had begun to appear almost dazzlingly beautiful to him. On these occasions he would lament his own unattractiveness, and would be overcome by the bitter realization that she was like a jewel dangling just beyond his reach. This was the woman who had just summoned him on the telephone.

He raced down the corridor, which was jammed with outpatients. As soon as he reached the main entrance of the hospital he caught sight of her pure white dress. Her tiny face looked as pale as that of a baby bird.

'You said you'd coughed up blood. About how much was there?'

'Around half a cup.'

Tuberculosis, he wondered, or just a simple case of bronchitis? In either case there was no need for concern; with the medical facilities available in the year 2005, treatment of these diseases had become as simple as twisting a baby's arm. At the very worst, she might have lung cancer, but that would be exceptional for someone her age.

'Have you felt like you've had a cold?'

'Yes, now that you mention it. These last couple of days.'

'Then there's nothing to worry about. You've simply got an inflammation of the bronchae,' Bontarō announced with a deliberately cheerful face. 'There's no need to consult your brother. I can fix you up myself. But shall we take some X-rays just to be on the safe side?'

'Where is Gōichi?'

'Probably at the Cancer Centre. It's Dr Inokuchi's day there, and he probably went along with him.'

Sayuri seemed anxious that her brother was not at the hospital, but she did as Bontarō instructed and followed him into No. 3 X-ray Room. He quickly drew up a chart and asked Iwamura, the X-ray technician, to take the pictures. Then he turned around and caught a glimpse of Sayuri's round white shoulder as she quietly began to undress. Flustered, he called, 'Well, thanks,' to Iwamura and headed down the corridor.

The sun shone warmly through the windows as an outpatient asked him directions to the examination room. Eventually Sayuri finished with the X-rays and came to see him, running her fingers through her tousled hair.

'Will I be all right?'

'What are you talking about? Of course you'll be all right. Even if it's TB, we're no longer living in the days when it took a year or two of treatment. They were grateful back then to have streptomycin to use. Now we don't even bother with drugs; we just burn up the afflicted area with electrical radiation. Recovery takes a mere two weeks.'

How happy he would be if a charming young woman like this were to love him, he thought. But that could never be. Sayuri would doubtless marry some wealthy young man.

The X-rays were ready in twenty minutes. Bontarō decided to show them to Dr Fukanuma, a chest specialist in Internal Medicine. His own eye could detect no abnormalities in the X-rays, but he wanted to get a second opinion.

'To me, your chest looks like that of a baby. But I'd like a distinguished physician to have a look at the pictures. Please wait here.'

Glancing at the X-rays that exposed her ribs and lungs for all to see, Sayuri blushed and nodded her head.

Dr Fukanuma was in Internal Medicine Laboratory No. 1, peering into a microscope. When he saw Bontarō he called, 'Hi!' Though they worked in different departments, Bontarō was fond of this burly doctor.

'Fine. I'll have a look at them.'

'From what I've seen, there aren't any cavities in the lung area. And there don't appear to be any shadows in the bronchial passages.'

'Ah-hah. Then it's probably a simple case of bronchitis.' As he peered at the lighted screen, Dr Fukanuma poked a cigarette into his mouth and lit it with his cigarette lighter. Then suddenly he put out the lighter and said softly, 'Wait a minute! What's this? This spot here near the heart . . . I don't like this. I don't like it at all.'

'Where, Doctor?'

Fukanuma looked searchingly at Bontarō's anxious face, then pointed to a spot on the X-ray with his stubby finger. It was smaller than a bean, a spot that on casual examination might be mistaken for a blood vessel.

'Doctor, is it cancer?'

'I think so. We'll need to do some more thorough tests, but . . .'

Fukanuma's diagnosis proved correct. The detailed examinations were performed by Bontarō and Sayuri's brother Gōichi, who came hurrying back to the hospital when he heard the news. The Eccleman Reaction was positive; the electronic brain scan came back positive—everything supported the diagnosis that the mucosa between the heart and lungs had been attacked by cancer. Unfortunately, since it lay in the region between the heart and lungs, the cancer was in the most precarious position, surgically speaking. I regret to have to inform you that, even in the year 2005, the only way to cure cancer was through surgery; I do, however, have an obligation to report the facts as they exist. I cannot tell a lie.

'Does Sayuri know about this?' Bontarō asked, a dismal expression on his face. He had never dreamed that his offhand diagnosis would be refuted by such grave findings.

'We've told her that it's tuberculosis. She doesn't know anything about medical science,' said Gōichi, his face stiff. 'At the moment she's resting peacefully in her room.'

'It's a dangerous operation. Do you want to go through with it?'

'What choice have we got? Father's agreed to it.'

Bontarō knew how hazardous this operation could be. To date, at K. University they had seen only two cases of lung cancer in this part of the body; in both instances surgery had failed. The patients had died on the operating table. Knowing this history, Bontarō could understand how Gōichi felt as he pondered his sister's chances for survival.

I must point out here that surgery in the year 2005 was nothing like the procedures you are familiar with today. In 1998, at the University of California, micro-gamma rays that could shrink objects to a fraction of their normal size were discovered; this led to a sweeping revolution in surgical technique. Dr Friedman was conducting research at the University on cancer-destroying rays, when one day he accidentally turned the No. 606 light-rays on his laboratory mice and went out for lunch. When he returned to his laboratory, he was astounded to find that the mice had shrunk to the size of fleas, and that the wire cage which contained them had been reduced to the size of a soya bean. This discovery had as profound an effect on the medical world as the discovery of penicillin and streptomycin, which began the antibiotic revolution of the 1940s.

For instance, surgeons no longer anaesthetized their patients and cut into their bodies and internal organs as they do today. When such antiquated methods are used, unsightly scars are left on the patient's body, even when extensive plastic surgery is done. Furthermore, it is a very serious matter to cut open the human body. How much more desirable to shrink the doctor to one-thousandth the size of a body – precisely half the size of a flea – have him slip inside the patient's body, cut out the infected areas from within, and then slip back out again. Not a single scar would remain. The patient could leave the hospital with a body as pristine as the one he had brought in before the operation.

The American film *Fantastic Voyage* was based upon this imaginary premise, but in Bontarō's day the procedure was no longer a fantasy. Dr Friedman's micro-gamma rays were being used far and wide throughout the Japanese medical world. Surgeons reduced to one-thousandth the size of the human body rode in proportionately-diminished submarines, and it was a routine chore for them to travel through the human body and do their operations from within.

Sayuri's surgery was scheduled for 3 October. Four doctors were set to perform the procedure: the operating surgeon would be Dr Inokuchi, said to be without peer among cancer specialists. His first assistant was to be Dr Hirano, his second assistants Bontarō and the patient's brother, Gōichi. In Bontarō's case, he had stepped forward and requested that he be allowed to participate. Naturally he was motivated by his undisclosed love for Sayuri.

'So you'll join us, will you?' After Dr Inokuchi gave his premission, Gōichi clutched Bontarō's hand and thanked him in a voice brimming with emotion.

It was a funny feeling, climbing inside the body of one's beloved. Consider for a moment how fascinating it would be to enter into the body of the woman you love and examine her stomach or her heart or her large intestines. As an assistant surgeon Bontarō had already entered the bodies of some twenty women patients, but this time he awoke each day with a tingly sort of feeling inside, and he could not force himself to remain dispassionately detached.

'I wonder if a woman as beautiful as Sayuri really does have a stomach? And intestines too?' Logic clearly dictated the answer, but to a man in Bontarō's state of mind it seemed remarkable that she could have such commonplace organs.

29 September: SS Reaction Tests; Cardiological Tests.

30 September: PTA Test.

One might think these are tests for the patient, but that is not so. They are tests for the doctors who will be performing the operation, to determine whether they have the strength to endure changes in atmospheric pressure within the patient's body. Bontarō and Gōichi naturally underwent these tests, and were given passing marks in the examination room.

On 2 October, Bontarō found time between his chores and his research to drop into Sayuri's room. Her aunt was just in the process of peeling some fruit for her.

'Well, tomorrow's the day!'

Sayuri, unaware that she was suffering from cancer and under the impression that she had tuberculosis, was not in particularly low spirits.

'I'm so embarrassed.'

'Why?'

'Well, after all, you and my brother will be going inside my body.'

'There's nothing to be embarrassed about. All you have to do is fall asleep for three hours, and we'll be inside you and finished off before you know what's happened.'

'How rude!'

Still, as he saw Sayuri blinking her eyes to ward off the sunlight that poured through the window, he thought how beautiful she was. Her aunt was the glamorous actress Yoshinaga Sayuri, who had enjoyed great popularity in the Japanese film world some fifty years earlier, and it was said that Sayuri was the very image of her.

'In any case, you set your mind at rest about tomorrow,' he said, leaving the room. With the gentle autumn sun stroking his shoulders, he felt happy.

3 October. 10 a.m. In Operating Theatre No. 27 at K. University, doctors and nurses wearing large white face-masks and gowns – and looking very much like astronauts – gazed gravely down at the body of Sayuri stretched out on the operating table. She had already been anaesthetized, and was as motionless as a wax doll.

'It's 10.05, isn't it?' The surgical team, led by Dr Inokuchi, nodded goodbye to the anaesthetist, the cardiologist and the nurses, and entered a separate chamber. This room was in fact an elevator. After thick doors had closed with a dull clatter, the entire chamber was filled with a purple radiating light. The micro-gamma rays were beginning to pour in from all directions.

With each passing second their bodies grew smaller, but they were unaware of the change, since they were all shrinking together.

The elevator began its descent underground. Down below a submarine twice the size of a flea was awaiting them.

The vessel was supplied with aqualungs and all the necessary surgical equipment. Gōichi, the patient's brother, had been selected to pilot the craft.

Once the four doctors had boarded the submarine, it was automatically sucked into a gigantic glass tube by a pneumatic inhalator. The glass tube was in reality the hypodermic syringe being used by the doctors up above.

In the United States microscopic-sized doctors were introduced into the patient's body through the eye duct, but in Japanese hospitals at Tokyo University, Keiō, and here at the K. University Medical Centre, they were sent along with the injection fluid into the patient's bloodstream, employing a technique discovered by Doctor Okazaki, a member of the Japan Academy. The injection fluid was scheduled to be shot into the patient's body at 10.30 a.m.; beside Dr Inokuchi, Bontarō started the countdown.

'Ten, nine, eight, seven . . .'

Soon they felt a minor shock, then a landscape like the surface of the moon opened up before their eyes. But it was not the surface of the moon; it was Sayuri's epidermis. They had arrived at the spot where they would be injected into her body. As far as they could see the area was thickly overgrown with what appeared to be reeds withered by the cold of winter; this was in fact the downy growth of hair on the surface of her skin.

Although he had already participated in twenty intravenous operations, on this occasion Bontarō was deeply moved. *Ah, so this is Sayuri's skin!* Careful that Inokuchi and Hirano did not observe him, Bontarō studied her epidermis with excitement in his eyes. A second shockwave. Churning bubbles of water thrashed about both sides of the vessel. At last they were being injected into the patient's body.

How can one describe the insider's view of the bloodstream that appeared momentarily outside the window of their submarine?

Lord Bagen-Saylor, who observed the very bottom of the ocean depths, wrote the following description in his book *The Mystery of the Sea*:

> I have never witnessed a realm as splendid, as sumptuous and dazzling as the bottom of the ocean. I had never known that a palace so magnificent could exist upon the face of this planet.

These words of Lord Bagen-Saylor can be applied to the view of the human body afforded to physicians in the year 2005. Inside the bloodstream, dancing about randomly overhead, were swarms of white and red corpuscles. It is true that here one cannot see the many colours of the fish that populate the depths of the ocean, but those who have once witnessed the ballet performed by these corpuscles can never forget the sight.

The sound they heard, like the intermittent beating of a drum, was the pounding of the heart. As they drew closer to the sound, the surgeons knew they were approaching the diseased area.

Objects like brown strands of seaweed floated by. These were human fatigue toxins, which are normally expelled from the body in the urine. The greater the number of these brown threads present, the stronger the indication that the subject was tired or that something was amiss in the body.

'There are a great many fatigue toxins, aren't there?' Dr Hirano said to Dr Inokuchi. Bontarō held his ear to the communicator which kept them in contact with the outside. The team of doctors in the operating theatre remained in constant touch with the submarine.

'Pulse – normal. Blood pressure – unchanged.' Bontarō announced the report to Dr Inokuchi in a loud voice. The doctor nodded vigorously and muttered, 'It's time to determine whether the cancer has spread beyond this region.'

The drum-like pounding of the heart grew still louder. They were at last nearing the afflicted zone.

'What's our velocity?' Gōichi reported their speed to Dr Hirano, who then pressed a button on top of the control panel. A screen set up inside the submarine displayed vividly enlarged X-ray photographs of the patient's lesions.

'Let's get ready.'

The four men removed their white gowns. Underneath their gowns they wore wet-suits and aqualungs. From a large box they removed a variety of instruments that looked like fire extinguishers. Among these instruments were several razor-sharp electronic scalpels that would cut away at the diseased area while spraying it with a mist of disinfectant.

For several minutes now their craft had been drifting alongside Sayuri's lungs, which looked like clusters of large pink balloons. Blood vessels criss-crossed the surface of these balloons like meshwork.

'Look at that!' Dr Inokuchi raised his hand and pointed. 'Already there's been a discoloration caused by the cancer cells.'

In one area the pink region had begun to fade, to be replaced by a disagreeably leaden coloration. As the X-rays had shown, cancer had spread from this point onto the mucilaginous zone extending to the heart.

'Stopping engines!' Gōichi shouted and pushed a button.

After consultation with Dr Inokuchi, Hirano gave instructions to the two younger assistants. 'We'll be cutting out a large portion starting at the B segment of the lower lung lobe. Is that clear?'

'I'll go first,' Dr Inokuchi announced, and with him at the head, the four left their craft. Their aqualungs swaying in the currents, and their oxygen inhalators clutched between their teeth, they swam through the bloodstream towards the infected area. Bontarō stayed in constant contact with the team of doctors above.

'How is the patient's condition?' He started to ask, 'How is Sayuri?' but caught himself.

'Satisfactory. Patient is sleeping soundly. No changes in pulse, blood pressure, or electrocardiogram,' came the reply from the operating theatre. It was time to begin the internal surgery.

'I shall start making the incision.' Thus began the doctors' difficult, painstaking task.

Two hours later, the fearsome cancer cells had all been cut away. To insure that there would be no reoccurrence in the scar tissue, a healthy dose of the powerful antibiotic ACM – discovered by Dr Umezawa at Tokyo University – was applied liberally to the wound with a giant atomizer.

'A clean cut!' Dr Hirano signalled triumphantly to Dr Inokuchi with his hand. The operation had gone without a hitch, and according to the information from above, the patient displayed virtually no dangerous after-effects.

'The way this looks, there seems very little chance of a relapse.'

'This will provide invaluable data for our medical department.'

When they returned to the submarine, the four surgeons removed their wet-suits and aqualungs, and sat down for a leisurely glass of whisky. The post-operative drink was especially delectable. The most appetizing whisky was that consumed after an operation had gone smoothly.

'Don't drink too much and get us into an accident,' Dr Hirano said jokingly to Gōichi, who responded, 'I'm really very grateful to all of you. Thanks to you my sister will get her health back.'

'She will indeed. Once she's back on her feet, you've got to find her a good husband.'

'When that time comes, I'll have to rely on you gentlemen for help once again.'

Bontarō listened to the casual banter between his three colleagues with a touch of melancholy. After today's success, Sayuri would be restored to normal health within two months. She would go back to the university. That beautiful, vibrant face would be walking down the streets of the city once more. But then she will have nothing more to do with me. The very thought grieved him.

'Well, let's head back.' Gōichi, unaware of the disposition of his friend's heart, slid into the driver's seat.

Inside the blood vessels visibility was poor. The quantity of blood cells had increased with the flow of blood from the surgical wound. The entire region was as blue as a sea of ink (as you may know, blood is not red; within the body, untouched by oxygen, it shone a vivid blue). Somewhat apprehensively, Dr Hirano asked Gōichi. 'Is everything all right?'

'Yes. Just fine, I think.'

They had travelled far enough that the density of the blood within the vessels should have been thinning a bit, but their field of vision still had not cleared. It was peculiar.

'Are you sure you didn't take a wrong turn somewhere?'

'I . . . don't think I did.'

But when the surrounding corpuscles began to decrease in number, they realized that their craft was nowhere near the pink-coloured pulmonary region, but was in fact advancing down some sort of passage with brownish, multi-pleated walls.

'Hey! Where are we?' Bontarō was first to notice the incongruity. The brown walls were contracting slightly, like some living thing, and emitting a great many objects that resembled thread ravellings. Before Bontarō realized what these were, Gōichi grasped the entire situation, and with a pale face, shouted, 'Hello! We're in the large intestine! Damnation! I never could hold my liquor, and with all the celebration over the success of Sayuri's operation, I've drunk too much whisky. Damn it!'

Just as drunken driving in an automobile was a misdemeanour in the 1980s, so was it unlawful in 2005 for a surgeon piloting through the human bloodstream to be under the influence.

'Can't we go back the way we came?' asked Dr Hirano, rising from his chair. But Gōichi shook his head.

'It's impossible. I'm sorry. As you know, there is no way to go against the current, given the air pressure that surges into the intestinal tract from the stomach.'

'All too true.'

'Doctor, I don't know how to apologize.'

'Don't worry about that; think of a way to get us out of here.'

'We can charge ahead through the intestine and get out by way of my sister's anus.'

'Good. We'll do it!'

Bontarō had participated in many internal operations, but this was the first time he had been inside the intestines. And to have to exit through the rectal opening . . .

So this . . .

A brownish liquid surrounded the craft. The rubbery mountains that were the inner walls of the intestine stretched ahead as far as the eye could see. It was like feeling one's way in the dark through a long tunnel.

So this is Sayuri's intestine!

He was moved beyond words. What a strange sensation to find himself inside the intestines of a woman he thought imcomparably beautiful! Within the body of this lovely woman were the same intestines and stomach that any ordinary person possessed. Although rationally he had always known this, until now he had not sensed the tangible reality of it all. But here it was right before his very eyes.

The long tunnel of intestines wound its way endlessly forward.

'Wait!' Something suddenly dawned on Dr Hirano, and he bounded from his chair. 'Before the operation, your sister did evacuate her bowels, didn't she?'

'Pardon?'

Realizing how Gōichi must feel, Hirano rephrased his question. 'What I mean to say is, the patient was cleaned out with an enema before surgery, wasn't she?'

'I . . . think so.' Gōichi was at pains to answer this question. But Dr Hirano's concern was not to be taken lightly. If in fact the intestines had not been irrigated, eventually their submarine would collide with the stool that blocked the end of Sayuri's alimentary canal. They had no way of knowing whether their miniscule vessel could penetrate such a mass.

'I'll check with the head nurses in the operating theatre.' Bontarō hurriedly picked up the communicator and brought it to his ear. Strangely, there was no response. The problem was not mechanical failure; just as radio waves grow indistinct high up in the mountains, the vital electric waves that flowed through the bloodstream could not reach the outside world from within the intestinal tract.

'Hello? Hello! Doctor, I can't get through!'

'You can't? Well, keep trying!'

Before long the fluid that enveloped the submarine began to be tinged with a markedly yellow colour. Apparently Dr Hirano's fears were being confirmed. The patient's bowels had not been evacuated before surgery.

'Do you think we could smash through a stool of ordinary consistency in this craft?'

'If it's on the diarrhetic side, there should be no problem. But if it's solid, there is no way we'll get through it.' Gōichi's head drooped. 'Doctor, please let me go outside the craft.'

'What would you do out there?'

'I'm embarrassed to have to say this, but my sister has always been plagued by constipation. I would imagine that up ahead we will find a remarkably solid stool.'

'Hmmm.'

'I shall therefore cut a hole in my sister's stool with the surgical scalpel. A hole just big enough for our ship to pass through.'

Bontarō could not stand by and let his friend undertake this formidable task alone. 'You can't do it by yourself. I'll go with you.'

'You will? Thank you! But you must be sure to wear your gas mask.'

Gas masks were kept on hand in the submarine in case unusually foul odours should sweep through the body. And they had to be prepared for the presence of noxious methane gas within the intestines. Bontarō and Gōichi donned their aqualungs once again and put on their gas masks; then, strapping oxygen cylinders to their backs, they left the submarine.

They swam through the cloudy yellow liquid. On and on they swam. Were this not Sayuri, even Bontarō would have turned back. Soon they rounded the second bend.

Ahead of them, an enormous grey object began sluggishly to move. Without warning, the grey figure detached itself from the intestinal wall and darted at the two men, twisting its body as if to attack them and swallow them up.

'Look out! A threadworm!'

'What? A threadworm?'

'Yes! A threadworm that's sucking all the nourishment out of your sister's intestines. Why didn't you give her some worm medicine?'

'We don't have time to argue about it. We'll kill it with our scalpels!'

They stabbed at the approaching threadworm with their surgical knives. A white fluid squirted out around them. Showing its sharp teeth, the worm writhed in agony. Two more thrusts, then three. It was a fight to the death between man and threadworm.

The battle was over in five minutes. Bontarō's arms were heavy with weariness, and for a few moments he was dazed. He thought of the summer two years before, when he and Sayuri had gone to Gōichi's summer cottage in Hayama and put on aqualungs to go spear-fishing. He couldn't understand why such a memory should surface at a time like this.

A solid black precipice loomed before them. They swam back and forth, jabbing at the obstruction with their scalpels. It had the consistency of clay, but seemed to be quite thick.

'Listen, at this rate it will take us more than a day to dig a hole large enough for the submarine. There's no alternative. I'll ask Dr Inokuchi and Dr Hirano to abandon ship.'

'Are you just going to leave the craft here in the intestines?'

'I'll give my sister a diarrhetic tomorrow and get her to excrete it.'

While Gōichi returned to the submarine, Bontarō plied his scalpel with all his might. After ten minutes all the feeling had gone out of his arms. 'Why didn't they give her an enema?' He cursed the careless nurses. He wanted to give them a good piece of his mind.

Suddenly a hole broke open in front of him. Fortunately his scalpel had been gouging away at the thinnest portion of the mass.

'I've done it!' Encouraged by his success, Bontarō dug in with increased vigour. At the same time, the figures of the two chief doctors – safely equipped with gas marks – could just be distinguished in the distance through the muddy liquid.

After passing through the large clay-like formation, the doctors at long last reached the tip of the alimentary canal. Yet here, too, an impasse they had not considered was awaiting them. Bontarō was the first to realize it. He looked around at the three masked men and said, 'Doctors, the anus isn't necessarily open all the time. In fact, speaking in strictly clinical terms, under ordinary circumstances it remains in a closed position. With our flagging energy, we will not be able to force our way through that orifice. We cannot make contact with the team outside. What shall we do?'

After struggling this far, they had no idea what to do next.

'We're almost out of oxygen.'

'How much is left?'

'We'll only last another ten minutes or less.'

The four men no longer had the energy to go back the way they had come. Unless something were done, however, Dr Inokuchi – the pride of the K. University Medical Centre – Dr Hirano, Gōichi and Bontarō would all die a miserable death in the faecal matter inside the intestines. A miserable shitty death.

To what end have I studied so diligently? Even if they did belong to Sayuri, how miserable to breathe his last here inside her intestines, thought Bontarō. It would grieve his mother back home to find out that her son had studied so hard only to meet with such an end. The face of his aged mother in the provinces darted across his mind.

'I have just one idea,' Dr Inokuchi, who had been silent up till now, said gravely.

'What is it, Doctor?'

'We'll make the patient fart.'

'Fart?'

'That is correct. If we cause the patient to pass wind, the anus will open. And we will be blown out by the rush of wind. This will of course place our bodies under considerable stress, but we'll just have to accept that. It's the only way.'

'Are you sure we won't get whiplash?'

'Listen, this is no time to be worrying about whiplash!'

'But, Doctor, how are we going to make her break wind?'

'We must all stimulate the inner wall of the intestine here. Use both hands and tickle it as hard as you can. I don't know whether it will work or not, but let's give it a try.'

The four doctors began to stroke the brown wall with their hands. They did their best to make it budge. But the wall, like a huge rocky cliff, did not even flinch.

'One more time!'

The second attempt also ended in failure. A third try fared no better.

'It's no good.'

'Just once more. If that doesn't work, we'll all join hands and die singing "At Sea Be My Body Water-soaked".'

As they tried a fourth time, their eyes began to swim. They had exhausted every resource of mind and body. Then, far in the distance, they heard Gōichi calling, 'Doctor, the intestine has started to move!' At that instant, Bontarō was swept up by ninety-mile-an-hour winds like those at the centre of a typhoon. As he lost consciousness, he knew he had been saved.

Five days later Bontarō was able to walk again, and that morning he summoned up the courage to visit Sayuri's room.

He was uneasy. He wondered whether he could still feel love for Sayuri after the experience he had gone through.

When he knocked on the door, he heard her charming voice. Dressed in a pale blue gown, she was eating some gelatin with the help of a nurse.

'How are you?'

'I'm fine. Thank you so much.'

Sayuri had no inkling of the route the doctors had used to exit from her body. That was a medical secret, something that could not be divulged to the patient.

'My, what's happened to you? Look at your face!'

Bontarō's face was covered with dark red bruises, souvenirs of the hurricane-strength winds that had struck him squarely in the face as he was whisked from her intestines.

'Oh, nothing. I got drunk and fell down the stairs.' Bontarō mustered a pained grin. Blissfully ignorant, Sayuri flashed her pearly-white teeth in surprise and said, 'What a stinker you are!'

Her face was stunning. One by one Bontarō recalled the experiences he had endured inside her intestines five days earlier – swimming out of the submarine with a gas mask on his face; the combat with the threadworm; breaking through the wall of clay. Despite it all, he thought she was beautiful. He knew he loved her. In the end love had won out over physiology.

'You're right. I'll be more careful from now on.'

He went out into the hallway, drinking deeply of the euphoria that rightfully belonged to a doctor in the year 2005. But then, seeing a patient restored to health is a great joy for a doctor in any day and age.

UNZEN

As he sat on the bus for Unzen, he drank a bottle of milk and gazed blankly at the rain-swept sea. The frosty waves washed languidly against the shore just beneath the coastal highway.

The bus had not yet left the station. The scheduled hour of departure had long since passed, but a connecting bus from Nagasaki still had not arrived, and their driver was chatting idly with the woman conductor and displaying no inclination to switch on the engine. Even so the tolerant passengers uttered no word of complaint, but merely pressed their faces against the window glass. A group of bathers from the hot springs walked by, dressed in large, thickly-padded kimonos. They shielded themselves from the rain with umbrellas borrowed from their inn. The counters of the gift shops were lined with all sorts of decorative shells and souvenir bean-jellies from the local hot springs, but there were no customers around to buy their wares.

'This place reminds me of Atagawa in Izu,' Suguro grumbled to himself as he snapped the cardboard top back onto the milk bottle. 'What a disgusting landscape.'

He had to chuckle a bit at himself for coming all the way to this humdrum spot at the western edge of Kyushu. In Tokyo he had not had the slightest notion that this village of Obama, home of many of the Christian martyrs and some of the participants in the Shimabara Rebellion, would be so commonplace a town.

From his studies of the Christian era in Japan, Suguro knew that around 1630 many of the faithful had made the climb from Obama towards Unzen, which a Jesuit of the day had called 'one of the tallest mountains in Japan'. The Valley of Hell high up on Unzen was an ideal place for torturing Christians. According to the records, after 1629, when the Nagasaki Magistrate Takenaka Shigetsugu hit upon the idea of abusing the Christians in this hot spring inferno, sixty or seventy prisoners a day were roped together and herded from Obama to the top of this mountain.

Now tourists strolled the streets of the village, and popular songs blared out from loudspeakers. Nothing remained to remind one of that sanguinary history. But precisely three centuries before the present month of January, on a day of misty rain, the man whose footsteps Suguro now hoped to retrace had undoubtedly climbed up this mountain from Obama.

Finally the engine started up, and the bus made its way through the village. They passed through a district of two- and three-storey Japanese inns, where men leaned with both hands on the railings of the balconies and peered down into the bus. Even those windows which were deserted were draped with pink and white washcloths and towels. When the bus finally passed beyond the hotel district, both sides of the mountain road were lined with old stone walls and squat farmhouses with thatched roofs.

Suguro had no way of knowing whether these walls and farmhouses had existed in the Christian century. Nor could he be sure that this road was the one travelled by the Christians, the officers, and the man he was pursuing. The only certain thing was that, during their fitful stops along the path, they had looked up at this same Mount Unzen wrapped in grey mist.

He had brought a number of books with him from Tokyo, but he now regretted not including a collection of letters from Jesuits of the day who had reported on the Unzen martyrdoms to their superiors in Rome. He had thoughtlessly tossed into his bag one book that would be of no use to him on this journey – Collado's *Christian Confessions*.

The air cooled as the bus climbed into the hills, and the passengers, peeling skins from the mikans they had bought at Obama, listened half-heartedly to the sing-song travelogue provided by the conductor.

'Please look over this way,' she said with a waxy smile. 'There are two large pine trees on top of the hill we are about to circle. It's said that at about this spot, the Christians of olden days would turn around and look longingly back at the village of Obama. These trees later became known as the Looking-Back Pines.'

Collado's *Christian Confessions* was published in Rome in 1632, just five years before the outbreak of the Shimabara Rebellion. By that time the shogunate's persecution of the Christians had grown fierce, but a few Portuguese and Italian missionaries had still managed to steal into Japan from Macao or Manila. The *Christian Confessions* were printed as a practical guide to Japanese grammar for the benefit of these missionaries. But what Suguro found hard to understand was why Collado had made public the confessions of these Japanese Christians, when a

Catholic priest was under no circumstances permitted to reveal the innermost secrets of the soul shared with him by members of his flock.

Yet the night he read the *Confessions*, Suguro felt as though a more responsive chord had been struck within him than with any other history of the Christian era he had encountered. Every study he had read was little more than a string of paeans to the noble acts of priests and martyrs and common believers inspired by faith. They were without exception chronicles of those who had sustained their beliefs and their testimonies no matter what sufferings or tortures they had to endure. And each time he read them, Suguro had to sigh, 'There's no way I can emulate people like this.'

He had been baptized as a child, along with the rest of his family. Since then he had passed through many vicissitudes and somehow managed to arrive in his forties without rejecting his religion. But that was not due to firm resolve or unshakeable faith. He was more than adequately aware of his own spiritual slovenliness and pusillanimity. He was certain that an unspannable gulf separated him from the ancient martyrs of Nagasaki, Edo and Unzen who had effected glorious martyr-doms. Why had they all been so indomitable?

Suguro diligently searched the Christian histories for someone like himself. But there was no one to be found. Finally he had stumbled across the *Christian Confessions* one day in a second-hand bookshop, and as he flipped indifferently through the pages of the book, he had been moved by the account of a man whose name Collado had concealed. The man had the same feeble will and tattered integrity as Suguro. Gradually he had formed in his mind an image of this man – genuflect-ing like a camel before the priest nearly three hundred years earlier, relishing the almost desperate experience of exposing his own filthiness to the eyes of another.

'I stayed for a long time with some heathens. I didn't want the innkeeper to realize I was a Christian, so I went with him often to the heathen temples and chanted along with them. Many times when they praised the gods and buddhas, I sinned greatly by nodding and agreeing with them. I don't remember how many times I did that. Maybe twenty or thirty times – more than twenty, anyway.

'And when the heathens and the apostates got together to slander us Christians and blaspheme against God, I was there with them. I didn't try to stop them talking or to refute them.

'Just recently, at the Shōgun's orders the Magistrate came to our fief from the capital, determined to make all the Christians here apostatize.

Everyone was interrogated and pressed to reject the Christian codes, or at least to apostatize in form only. Finally, in order to save the lives of my wife and children, I told them I would abandon my beliefs.'

Suguro did not know where this man had been born, or what he had looked like. He had the impression he was a samurai, but there was no way to determine who his master might have been. The man would have had no inkling that his private confession would one day be published in a foreign land, and eventually fall into the hands of one of his own countrymen again, to be read by a person like Suguro. Though he did not have a clear picture of how the man looked, Suguro had some idea of the assortment of facial expressions he would have had to employ in order to evade detection. If he had been born in that age, Suguro would have had no qualms about going along with the Buddhist laymen to worship at their temples, if that meant he would not be exposed as a Christian. When someone mocked the Christian faith, he would have lowered his eyes and tried to look unconcerned. If so ordered, he might even have written out an oath of apostasy, if that would mean saving the lives of his family as well as his own.

A faint ray of light tentatively penetrated the clouds that had gathered over the summit of Unzen. Maybe it will clear up, he thought. In summer this paved road would no doubt be choked by a stream of cars out for a drive, but now there was only the bus struggling up the mountain with intermittent groans. Groves of withered trees shivered all around. A cluster of rain-soaked bungalows huddled silently among the trees, their doors tightly shut.

'Listen, martyrdom is no more than a matter of pride.'

He had had this conversation in the corner of a bar in Shinjuku. A pot of Akita salted-fish broth simmered in the centre of the *sake*-stained table. Seated around the pot, Suguro's elders in the literary establishment had been discussing the hero of a novel he had recently published. The work dealt with some Christian martyrs in the 1870s. The writers at the gathering claimed that they could not swallow the motivations behind those martyrdoms the way Suguro had.

'At the very core of this desire to be a martyr you'll find pride, pure and simple.'

'I'm sure pride plays a part in it. Along with the desire to become a hero, and even a touch of insanity, perhaps. But –'

Suguro fell silent and clutched his glass. It was a simple task to pinpoint elements of heroism and pride among the motives for martyr-dom. But when those elements were obliterated residual motives still remained. Those residual motives were of vital importance.

'Well, if you're going to look at it that way, you can find pride and selfishness underlying virtually every human endeavour, every single act of good faith.'

In the ten years he had been writing fiction, Suguro had grown increasingly impatient with those modern novelists who tried to single out the egotism and pride in every act of man. To Suguro's mind, such a view of humanity entailed the loss of something of consummate value, like water poured through a sieve.

The road wound its way to the summit through dead grass and barren woods. In days past, lines of human beings had struggled up this path. Both pride and madness had certainly been part of their make-up, but there must have been something more to it.

'The right wing during the war, for instance, had a certain martyr mentality. I can't help thinking there's something impure going on when people are intoxicated by something like that. But perhaps I feel that way because I experienced the war myself,' one of his elders snorted as he drank down his cup of tepid *sake*. Sensing an irreconcilable mis-understanding between himself and this man, Suguro could only grin acquiescently.

Before long he caught sight of a column of white smoke rising like steam from the belly of the mountain. Though the windows of the bus were closed, he smelled a faintly sulphuric odour. Milky white crags and sand came into clear focus.

'Is that the Valley of Hell?'

'No.' The conductor shook her head. 'It's a little further up.'

A tiny crack in the clouds afforded a glimpse of blue sky. The bus, which up until now had panted along, grinding its gears, suddenly seemed to catch its breath and picked up speed. The road had levelled off, then begun to drop. A series of arrows tacked to the leafless trees, apparently to guide hikers, read 'Valley of Hell'. Just ahead was the red roof of the rest-house.

Suguro did not know whether the man mentioned in the *Confessions* had come here to the Valley of Hell. But, as if before Suguro's eyes, the image of another individual had overlapped with that of the first man and now stumbled along with his head bowed. There was a little more detailed information about this second man. His name was Kichijirō, and he first appeared in the historical records on the fifth day of

December, 1631, when seven priests and Christians were tortured at the Valley of Hell. Kichijirō came here to witness the fate of the fathers who had cared for him. He had apostatized much earlier, so he had been able to blend in with the crowd of spectators. Standing on tiptoe, he had witnessed the cruel punishments which the officers inflicted on his spiritual mentors.

Father Christovao Ferreira, who later broke under torture and left a filthy smudge on the pages of Japanese Christian history, sent to his homeland a letter vividly describing the events of that day. The seven Christians arrived at Obama on the evening of December the second, and were driven up the mountain all the following day. There were several look-out huts on the slope, and that evening the seven captives were forced into one of them, their feet and hands still shackled. There they awaited the coming of dawn.

'The tortures commenced on the fifth of December in the following manner. One by one each of the seven was taken to the brink of the seething pond. There they were shown the frothy spray from the boiling water, and ordered to renounce their faith. The air was chilly and the hot water of the pond churned so furiously that, had God not sustained them, a single look would have cause them to faint away. They all shouted, "Torture us! We will not recant!" At this response, the guards stripped the garments from the prisoners' bodies and bound their hands and feet. Four of them held down a single captive as a ladle holding about a quarter of a litre was filled with the boiling water. Three ladlesful were slowly poured over each body. One of the seven, a young girl called Maria, fainted from the excruciating pain and fell to the ground. In the space of thirty-three days, each of them was subjected to this torture a total of six times.'

Suguro was the last one off when the bus came to a stop. The cold, taut mountain air blew a putrid odour into his nostrils. White steam poured onto the highway from the tree-ringed valley.

'How about a photograph? Photographs, anyone?' a young man standing beside a large camera on a tripod called out to Suguro. 'I'll pay the postage wherever you want to send it.'

At various spots along the road stood women proffering eggs in baskets and waving clumsily-lettered signs that read 'Boiled Eggs'. They too touted loudly for business.

Weaving their way among these hawkers, Suguro and the rest of the group from the bus walked towards the valley. The earth, overgrown with shrubbery, was virtually white, almost the colour of flesh stripped clean of its layer of skin. The rotten-smelling steam gushed ceaselessly from amid the trees. The narrow path stitched its way back and forth between springs of hot, bubbling water. Some parts of the white-speckled pools lay as calm and flat as a wall of plaster; others eerily spewed up slender sprays of gurgling water. Here and there on the hillocks formed from sulphur flows stood pine trees scorched red by the heat.

The bus passengers extracted boiled eggs from their paper sacks and stuffed them into their mouths. They moved forward like a column of ants.

'Come and look over here. There's a dead bird.'

'So there is. I suppose the gas fumes must have asphyxiated it.'

All he knew for certain was that Kichijirō had been a witness to those tortures. Why had he come? There was no way of knowing whether he had joined the crowd of Buddhist spectators in the hope of rescuing the priests and the faithful who were being tormented. The only tangible piece of information he had about Kichijirō was that he had forsworn his religion to the officers, 'so that his wife and children might live'. Nevertheless, he had followed in the footsteps of those seven Christians, walking all the way from Nagasaki to Obama, then trudging to the top of the bitterly cold peak of Unzen.

Suguro could almost see the look on Kichijirō's face as he stood at the back of the crowd, furtively watching his former companions with the tremulous gaze of a dog, then lowering his eyes in humiliation. That look was very like Suguro's own. In any case, there was no way Suguro could stand in chains before these loathsomely bubbling pools and make any show of courage.

A momentary flash of white lit up the entire landscape; then a fierce eruption burst forth with the smell of noxious gas. A mother standing near the surge quickly picked up her crouching child and retreated. A placard reading 'Dangerous Beyond This Point' was thrust firmly into the clay. Around it the carcasses of three dead swallows were stretched out like mummies.

This must be the spot where the Christians were tortured, he thought. Through a crack in the misty, shifting steam, Suguro saw the black outlines of a cross. Covering his nose and mouth with a handkerchief and balancing precariously near the warning sign, he peered below him. The mottled water churned and sloshed before his eyes. The Christians must have stood just where he was standing now when they were tortured. And Kichijirō would have stayed behind, standing about where the mother and her child now stood at a cautious distance, watching the spectacle with the rest of the crowd. Inwardly, did he ask them to forgive him? Had Suguro been in his shoes, he would have had no recourse but to repeat over and over again, 'Forgive me! I'm not strong enough to be a martyr like you. My heart melts just to think about this dreadful torture.'

Of course, Kichijirō could justify his attitude. If he had lived in a time of religious freedom, he would never have become an apostate. He might not have qualified for sainthood, but he could have been a man who tamely maintained his faith. But to his regret, he had been born in an age of persecution, and out of fear he had tossed away his beliefs. Not everyone can become a saint or a martyr. Yet must those who do not qualify as saints be branded forever with the mark of the traitor? – Perhaps he had made such a plea to the Christians who vilified him. Yet, despite the logic of his argument, he surely suffered pangs of remorse and cursed his own faint resolve.

'The apostate endures a pain none of you can comprehend.'

Over the span of three centuries this cry, like the shriek of a wounded bird, reached Suguro's ears. That single line recorded in the *Christian Confessions* cut at Suguro's chest like a sharp sword. Surely those were the words Kichijirō must have shouted to himself here at Unzen as he looked upon his tormented friends.

They reboarded the bus. The ride from Unzen to Shimabara took less than an hour. A fistful of blue finally appeared in the sky, but the air remained cold. The same conductor forced her usual smile and commented on the surroundings in a sing-song voice.

The seven Christians, refusing to bend to the tortures at Unzen, had been taken down the mountain to Shimabara, along the same route Suguro was now following. He could almost see them dragging their scalded legs, leaning on walking-sticks and enduring lashes from the officers.

Leaving some distance between them, Kichijirō had timorously followed behind. When the weary Christians stopped to catch their breath, Kichijirō also halted, a safe distance behind. He hurriedly crouched down like a rabbit in the overgrowth, lest the officers suspect him, and did not rise again until the group had resumed their trek. He was like a jilted woman plodding along in pursuit of her lover.

Half-way down the mountain he had a glimpse of the dark sea. Milky clouds veiled the horizon; several wan beams of sunlight filtered through the cracks. Suguro thought how blue the ocean would appear on a clear day.

'Look – you can see a blur out there that looks like an island. Unfortunately, you can't see it very well today. This is Dangō Island, where Amakusa Shirō, the commander of the Christian forces, planned the Shimabara Rebellion with his men.'

At this the passengers took a brief, apathetic glance towards the island. Before long the view of the distant sea was blocked by a forest of trees.

What must those seven Christians have felt as they looked at this ocean? They knew they would soon be executed at Shimabara. The corpses of martyrs were swiftly reduced to ashes and cast upon the seas. If that were not done, the remaining Christians would surreptitiously worship the clothing and even locks of hair from the martyrs as though they were holy objects. And so the seven, getting their first distant view of the ocean from this spot, must have realized that it would be their grave. Kichijirō too would have looked at the sea, but with a different kind of sorrow – with the knowledge that the strong ones in the world of faith were crowned with glory, while the cowards had to carry their burdens with them throughout their lives.

When the group reached Shimabara, four of them were placed in a cell barely three feet tall and only wide enough to accommodate one tatami. The other three were jammed into another room equally cramped. As they awaited their punishment, they persistently encouraged one another and went on praying. There is no record of where Kichijirō stayed during this time.

The village of Shimabara was dark and silent. The bus came to a stop by a tiny wharf where the rickety ferry-boat to Amakusa was moored forlornly. Wood chips and flotsam bobbed on the small waves that lapped at the breakwater. Among the debris floated an object that resembled a rolled-up newspaper; it was the corpse of a cat.

The town extended in a thin band along the seafront. The fences of local factories stretched far into the distance, while the odour of chemicals wafted all the way to the highway.

Suguro set out towards the reconstructed Shimabara Castle. The only signs of life he encountered along the way were a couple of high-school girls riding bicycles.

'Where is the execution ground where the Christians were killed?' he asked them.

'I didn't know there was such a place,' said one of them, blushing. She turned to her friend. 'Have you heard of anything like that? You don't know, do you?' Her friend shook her head.

He came to a neighbourhood identified as a former samurai residence. It had stood behind the castle, where several narrow paths intersected. A crumbling mud wall wound its way between the paths. The drainage ditch was as it had been in those days. Summer mikans poked their heads above the mud wall, which had already blocked out the evening sun. All the buildings were old, dark and musty. They had probably been the residence of a low-ranking samurai, built at the end of the Tokugawa period. Many Christians had been executed at the Shimabara grounds, but Suguro had not come across any historical documents identifying the location of the prison.

He retraced his steps, and after a short walk came out on a street of shops where popular songs were playing. The narrow street was packed with a variety of stores, including gift shops. The water in the drainage ditch was as limpid as water from a spring.

'The execution ground? I know where that is.' The owner of a tobacco shop directed Suguro to a pond just down the road. 'If you go straight on past the pond, you'll come to a nursery school. The execution ground was just to the side of the school.'

Though they say nothing of how he was able to do it, the records indicate that Kichijirō was allowed to visit the seven prisoners on the day before their execution. Possibly he put some money into the hands of the officers.

Kichijirō offered a meagre plate of food to the prisoners, who were prostrate from their ordeal.

'Kichijirō, did you retract your oath?' one of the captives asked compassionately. He was eager to know if the apostate had finally informed the officials that he could not deny his faith. 'Have you come here to see us because you have retracted?'

Kichijirō looked up at them timidly and shook his head.

'In any case, Kichijirō, we can't accept this food.'

'Why not?'

'Why not?' The prisoners were mournfully silent for a moment. 'Because we have already accepted the fact that we will die.'

Kichijirō could only lower his eyes and say nothing. He knew that he himself could never endure the sort of agony he had witnessed at the Valley of Hell on Unzen.

Through his tears he whimpered, 'If I can't suffer the same pain as you, will I be unable to enter Paradise? Will God forsake someone like me?'

He walked along the street of shops as he had been instructed and came to the pond. A floodgate blocked the overflow from the pond, and the water poured underground and into the drainage ditch in the village. Suguro read a sign declaring that the purity of the water in Shimabara village was due to the presence of this pond.

He heard the sounds of children at play. Four or five young children were tossing a ball back and forth in the nursery school playground. The setting sun shone feebly on the swings and sandbox in the yard. He walked around behind a drooping hedge of rose bushes and located the remains of the execution ground, now the only barren patch within a grove of trees.

It was a deserted plot some three hundred square yards in size, grown rank with brown weeds; pines towered over a heap of refuse. Suguro had come all the way from Tokyo to have a look at this place. Or had he made the journey out of a desire to understand better Kichijirō's emotions as he stood in this spot?

The following morning the seven prisoners were hoisted onto the unsaddled horses and dragged through the streets of Shimabara to this execution ground.

One of the witnesses to the scene has recorded the events of the day: 'After they were paraded about, they arrived at the execution ground, which was surrounded by a palisade. They were taken off their horses and made to stand in front of stakes set three metres apart. Firewood was already piled at the base of the stakes, and straw roofs soaked in sea water had been placed on top of them to prevent the flames from raging too quickly and allowing the martyrs to die with little agony. The ropes that bound them to the stakes were tied as loosely as possible, to permit them, up to the very moment of death, to twist their bodies and cry out that they would abandon their faith.

'When the officers began setting fire to the wood, a solitary man broke through the line of guards and dashed towards the stakes. He was shouting something, but I could not hear what he said over the roar of the fires. The fierce flames and smoke prevented the man from approaching the prisoners. The guards swiftly apprehended him and asked if he was a Christian. At that, the man froze in fear, and jabbering, "I am no Christian. I have nothing to do with these people! I just lost my head in all the excitement," he skulked away. But some in the crowd had seen him at the rear of the assemblage, his hands pressed together as he repeated over and over, "Forgive me! Forgive me!"

'The seven victims sang a hymn until the flames enveloped their stakes. Their voices were exuberant, totally out of keeping with the cruel punishment they were even then enduring. When those voices suddenly ceased, the only sound was the dull crackling of wood. The man who had darted forward could be seen walking lifelessly away from the execution ground. Rumours spread through the crowd that he too had been a Christian.'

Suguro noticed a dark patch at the very centre of the execution ground. On closer inspection he discovered several charred stones half buried beneath the black earth. Although he had no way of knowing whether these stones had been used here three hundred years before, when seven Christians had been burned at the stake, he hurriedly snatched up one of the stones and put it in his pocket. Then, his spine bent like Kichijirō's, he walked back towards the road.

MOTHERS

I reached the dock at nightfall.

The ferry-boat had not yet arrived. I peered over the low wall of the quay. Small grey waves laden with refuse and leaves licked at the jetty like a puppy quietly lapping up water. A single truck was parked in the vacant lot by the dock; beyond the lot stood two warehouses. A man had lit a bonfire in front of one of the warehouses; the red flames flickered.

In the waiting-room, five or six local men wearing high boots sat patiently on benches, waiting for the ticket booth to open. At their feet were dilapidated trunks and boxes loaded with fish. I also noticed several cages packed full of chickens. The birds thrust their long necks through the wire mesh and writhed as though in pain. The men sat quietly on the benches, occasionally glancing in my direction.

I felt as though I had witnessed a scene like this in some Western painting. But I couldn't recall who had sketched it, or when I had seen it.

The lights on the broad grey shore of the island across the water twinkled faintly. Somewhere a dog was howling, but I couldn't tell whether it was over on the island or here on my side of the bay.

Gradually some of the lights which I had thought belonged to the island began to move. I finally realized that they belonged to the ferry-boat that was heading this way. At last the ticket booth opened, and the men got up from the benches and formed a queue. When I lined up behind them, the smell of fish was overpowering. I had heard that most of the people on the island mixed farming with fishing.

Their faces all looked the same. Their eyes seemed sunken, perhaps because of the protruding cheekbones; their faces were void of expression, as if they were afraid of something. In short, dishonesty and dread had joined together to mould the faces of these islanders. Perhaps I felt that way because of the preconceived notions I had about the island I was about to visit. Throughout the Edo period, the residents of the island had suffered through poverty, hard, grinding labour and religious persecution.

After some time I boarded the ferry-boat, which soon pulled away from the harbour. Only three trips a day connected the island with the Kyushu mainland. Until just two years before, boats had made the crossing only twice a day, once in the morning and once in the evening.

It was in fact little more than a large motor launch and had no seats. The passengers stood between bicycles and fish crates and old trunks, exposed to the chilling sea winds that blew through the windows. Had this been Tokyo, some passengers would undoubtedly have complained at the conditions, but here no one said a word. The only sound was the grinding of the boat's engine; even the chickens in the cages at our feet did not utter a peep. I jabbed at some of the chickens with the tip of my shoe. A look of fear darted across their faces. They looked just like the men from the waiting-room, and I had to smile.

The wind whipped up; the sea was dark, and the waves black. I tried several times to light a cigarette, but the wind extinguished my match at every attempt. The unlit cigarette grew damp from my lips, and finally I hurled it overboard . . . though the winds may very well have blown it back onto the boat. The weariness of the twelve-hour bus-ride from Nagasaki overcame me. I was stiff from the small of my back to my shoulders. I closed my eyes and listened to the droning of the engine.

Several times, out on the pitch-black ocean, the pounding of the engine grew suddenly faint. In an instant it would surge up again, only to slacken once more. I listened to that process repeat itself several times before I opened my eyes again. The lights of the island were directly ahead.

'Hello!' a voice called. 'Is Watanabe there? Throw the line!'

There was a dull, heavy thud as the line was thrown to the quay.

I got off after the locals had disembarked. The cold night wind bore the smells of fish and of the sea. Just beyond the dock gate stood five or six shops selling dried fish and local souvenirs. I had heard that the best-known local product was a dried flying-fish called *ago*. A man dressed in boots and wearing a jacket stood in front of the shops. He watched me closely as I stepped through the gate, then came up to me and said, 'Sensei, thank you for coming all this way. The church sent me to meet you.'

He bowed to me an embarrassing number of times, then tried to wrest my suitcase from my hands. No matter how often I refused, he would not let go of it. The palms that brushed against my hand were as solid and large as the root of a tree. They were not like the soft, damp hands of the Tokyo Christians that I knew so well.

I tried to walk beside him, but he stubbornly maintained a distance of one pace behind me. I remembered that he had called me 'Sensei', and I felt bewildered. If the church people persisted in addressing me in terms of respect, the locals might be put on their guard against me.

The smell of fish that permeated the harbour trailed persistently after us. That odour seemed to have imbedded itself in the low-roofed houses and the narrow road over the course of many years. Off to my left, across the sea, the lights of Kyushu now shone faintly in the darkness.

'How is the Father?' I asked. 'I came as soon as I got his letter . . .'

But there was no answer from behind. I tried to detect whether I had done something to offend him, but that did not appear to be the case. Perhaps he was just diffident and determined not to engage in idle chatter. Or possibly, after long years of experience, the people of this island had concluded that the best way to protect themselves was to avoid imprudent conversation.

I had met their priest in Tokyo. He had come up from Kyushu to attend a meeting just after I had published a novel about the Christian era in Japan. I went up and introduced myself to him. He too had the deep-set eyes and the prominent cheekbones of the island's fishermen. Bewildered perhaps to be in Tokyo among all the notable clerics and nuns, his face tightened and he said very little when I spoke to him. In that sense, he was very much like the man who was now carrying my suitcase.

'Do you know Father Fukabori?' I had asked the priest. A year earlier, I had taken a bus to a fishing village an hour from Nagasaki. There I met the village priest, Father Fukabori, who was from the Urakami district. Not only did he teach me how to deep-sea fish, he also provided me with considerable assistance in my research. The purpose of my visit had been to visit the *kakure*, descendants of some of the original Christian converts in the seventeenth century who had, over the space of many years, gradually corrupted the religious practices. Father Fukabori took me to the homes of several of the *kakure*, who still stubbornly refused to be reconverted to Catholicism. As I have said, the faith of the *kakure* Christians over the long years of national isolation had drifted far from true Christianity and had embraced elements of Shinto, Buddhism and local superstition. Because of this, one of the missions of the Church in this region, ever since the arrival of Father Petitjean in the Meiji period, was the reconversion of the *kakure* who were scattered throughout the Gotō and Ikitsuki Islands.

'He let me stay at his church.' I continued to grasp for threads of conversation, but the priest clutched his glass of juice tightly and muttered only monosyllabic responses.

'Are there any *kakure* in your parish?'

'Yes.'

'They're starting to show up on television these days, and they look a little happier now that they're making some money out of it. The old man that Father Fukabori introduced me to was just like an announcer on a variety show. Is it easy to meet the *kakure* on your island?'

'No, it's very difficult.'

Our conversation broke off there, and I moved on in search of more congenial company.

Yet, to my surprise, a month ago I received a letter from this artless country priest. It opened with the customary Catholic 'Peace of the Lord' salutation and went on to say that he had persuaded some of the *kakure* who lived in his parish to show me their religious icons and copies of their prayers. His handwriting was surprisingly fluent.

I looked back at the man walking behind me and asked, 'Are there any *kakure* around here?'

He shook his head. 'No, they all live in the mountains.'

Half an hour later we reached the church. A man dressed in a black cassock, his hands clasped behind him, stood at the doorway. Beside him was a young man with a bicycle.

Since I had already met the priest – though only once – I greeted him casually, but he looked somewhat perplexed and glanced at the other two men. I had been thoughtless. I had forgotten that, unlike Tokyo or Osaka, in this district the priest was like a village headman, or in some cases as highly respected as a feudal lord.

'Jirō, go and tell Mr Nakamura that the Sensei has arrived,' he ordered. With a deep bow the young man climbed on his bicycle and disappeared into the darkness.

'Which way is the *kakure* village?' I asked. The priest pointed in the opposite direction to that from which I had come. I couldn't see any lights, perhaps because the mountains obstructed my view. In the age of persecution, to escape the eyes of the officials, the *kakure* Christians had settled as much as possible in secluded mountain fastnesses or on inaccessible coastlines. Undoubtedly that was the case here. We'll have to walk quite a way tomorrow, I thought, surveying my own rather fragile body. Seven years before, I had undergone chest surgery, and though I had recovered, I still had little faith in my physical strength.

I dreamed of my mother. In my dream I had just been brought out of the operating theatre, and was sprawled out on my bed like a corpse. A rubber tube connected to an oxygen tank was thrust into my nostril, and intravenous needles pierced my right arm and leg, carrying blood from the transfusion bottles dangling over my bed.

Although I should have been half unconscious, through the languid weight of the anaesthetic I recognized the grey shadow that held my hand. It was my mother. Strangely, neither my wife nor any of the doctors was in the room.

I have had that dream many times. Frequently I wake up unable to distinguish dream from reality and lie in a daze on my bed, until I realize with a sigh that I am not in the hospital where I spent three years, but in my own home.

I have not told my wife about that dream. She was the one who watched over me through every night after each of my three operations, and I felt remorseful that my wife did not even seem to exist in my dreams. The main reason I said nothing to her, however, was my distasteful realization that the firm bonds between my mother and myself – stronger than even I had suspected – continued to link us some twenty years after her death, even in my dreams.

I know little about psychoanalysis, so I have no idea exactly what this dream means. In it, I cannot actually see my mother's face. Nor are her movements distinct. When I reflect back on the dream, the figure seems to be my mother, but I cannot positively say that it is. But it most definitely is not my wife or any kind of nurse or attendant, or even a doctor.

So far as my memory serves me, I can recollect no experience in my youth when I lay ill in bed with my mother holding my hand. Normally the image of my mother that pops into my mind is the figure of a woman who lived her life fervently.

When I was five years old, we were living in Dairen in Manchuria in connection with my father's work. I can still vividly recall the icicles that hung down past the windows of our tiny house like the teeth of a fish. The sky is overcast, and it looks as if it will begin to snow at any moment, but the snow never comes. In a nine-by-twelve room my mother is practising the violin. For hours on end she practises the same melody over and over again. With the violin wedged under her chin, her face is hard, stone-like, and her eyes are fixed on a single point in space as she seems to be trying to isolate that one true note somewhere in the void. Unable to find that elusive note, she heaves a sigh; her irritation mounts, and she continues to scrape the bow across the strings. The brownish callouses on her chin were familiar to me. They had formed when she was still a student at the music academy and had kept her violin tucked constantly under her chin. The tips of her fingers, too, were as hard to the touch as pebbles, the result of the many thousands of times she had pressed down on the strings in her quest for that one note.

The image of my mother in my school-days – that image within my heart was of a woman abandoned by her husband. She sits like a stone statue on the sofa in that dark room at nightfall in Dairen. As a child I could not bear to see her struggling so to endure her grief. I sat near her, pretending to do my homework but concentrating every nerve in my body on her. Because I could not fathom the complex situation, I was all the more affected by the picture of her suffering, her hand pressed against her forehead. I was in torment, not knowing what I should do.

Those dismal days stretched from autumn into winter. Determined not to see her sitting in that darkened room, I walked home from school as slowly as I could. I followed the old White Russian who sold Russian bread everywhere he went. Around sunset I finally turned towards home, kicking pebbles along the side of the road.

One day, when my father had taken me out on one of our rare walks together, he said suddenly, 'Your mother . . . she's going back to Japan on an important errand. . . . Would you like to go with her?'

Detecting a grown-up's lie, I grunted, 'Uh-huh,' and went on walking along behind him in silence, kicking at every rock I could find. The following month, with financial assistance from her older sister in Kobe, my mother took me back to Japan.

And then my mother during my middle-school days. Though I have various memories of her, they all congeal on one spot. Just as she had once played her violin in search of the one true note, she subsequently adopted a stern, solitary life in quest of the one true religion. On wintry mornings, at the frozen fissure of dawn, I often noticed a light in her room. I knew what she was doing in there. She was fingering the beads of her rosary and praying. Eventually she would take me with her on the first Hankyū-line train of the day and set out for Mass. On the deserted train I slouched back in my seat and pretended to be rowing a boat. But occasionally I would open my eyes and see my mother's fingers gliding along those rosary beads.

In the darkness, I opened my eyes to the sound of rain. I dressed hurriedly and ran from my bungalow to the brick chapel across the way.

The chapel was almost too ornate for this beggarly island village. The previous evening, the priest had told me that the village Christians had worked for two years to erect this chapel, hauling the stones and cutting the wood themselves. They say that three hundred years ago, the faithful also built churches with their own hands to please the foreign missionaries. That custom has been passed down undiluted on this remote island off Kyushu.

In the dimly-lit chapel knelt three peasant women in their work attire, with white cloths covering their heads. There were also two men in working clothes. Since the nave was bereft of kneelers or benches, they each knelt on straw mats to offer up their prayers. One had the impression that, as soon as Mass was over, they would pick up their hoes and head straight for the fields or the sea. At the altar, the priest turned his sunken eyes towards the tiny congregation, lifted up the chalice with both hands and intoned the prayer of Consecration. The light from the candles illuminated the text of the large Latin missal. I thought of my mother. I couldn't help but feel that this chapel somehow resembled the church she and I had attended thirty years before.

When we stepped outside after Mass the rain had stopped, but a dense fog had settled in. The direction in which the *kakure* village lay was shrouded in a milky haze; the silhouettes of trees hovered like ghosts amid the fog.

'It doesn't look like you'll be able to set out in all this fog,' the priest muttered from behind me, rubbing his hands together. 'The mountain roads are very slippery. You'd better spend the day resting yourself. Why don't you go tomorrow?'

He proposed a tour of the Christian graves in his village for the afternoon. Since the *kakure* district lay deep in the mountains, it would be no easy matter for even a local resident to make the climb, and with only one lung I certainly did not have the strength to walk there in the dense, soaking mist.

Through breaks in the fog, the ocean appeared, black and cold. Not a single boat had ventured out. Even from where I stood, I could make out the frothy white fangs of the waves.

I had breakfast with the priest and went to lie down in the six-mat room that had been provided for me. In bed I reread a book about the history of this region. A thin rain began to fall; its sound, like shifting sands, deepened the solitude within my room, which was bare except for a bus timetable tacked to the wall. Suddenly I wanted to go back to Tokyo.

According to the historical documents, the persecution of Christians in this area commenced in 1607 and was at its fiercest between 1615 and 1617.

> Father Pedro de San Dominico
> Matthias
> Francisco Gorosuke
> Miguel Shin'emon
> Dominico Kisuke

This list includes only the names of the priests and monks who were martyred in the village in 1615. No doubt there were many more nameless peasants and fisherwomen who gave up their lives for the faith. In the past, as I devoted my free time to reading the history of Christian martyrdoms in Japan, I formulated within my mind an audacious theory. My hypothesis is that these public executions might have been carried out as warnings to the leaders of each village rather than to each individual believer. This will, of course, never be anything more than my own private conjecture so long as the historical records offer no supportive evidence. But I can't help feeling that the faithful in those days, rather than deciding individually whether to die for the faith or to apostatize, were instead bowing to the will of the entire community.

It has been my long-held supposition that, because the sense of community, based on blood relationships, was so much stronger among villagers in those days, it was not left up to individuals to determine whether they would endure persecution or succumb. Instead this matter was decided by the village as a whole. In other words, the officials, knowing that they would be exterminating their labour force if they executed an entire community that stubbornly clung to its faith, would only kill selected representatives of the village. In cases where there was no choice but apostasy, the villagers would renounce their beliefs en masse to ensure the preservation of the community. That, I felt, was the

fundamental distinction between Japanese Christian martyrdoms and
the martyrs in foreign lands.

The historical documents clearly indicate that in former times, nearly
fifteen hundred Christians lived on this ten-by-three-and-a-half-
kilometre island. The most active proselytizer on the island in those
days was the Portuguese father Camillo Constanzo, who was burned at
the stake on the beach of Tabira in 1622. They say that even after the fire
was lit and his body was engulfed in black smoke, the crowd could hear
him singing the *Laudate Dominum*. When he finished singing, he cried
'Holy! Holy!' five times and breathed his last.

Peasants and fishermen found to be practising Christianity were
executed on a craggy islet – appropriately named the Isle of Rocks – about
a half hour from here by rowing-boat. They were bound hand and foot,
taken to the top of the sheer precipice of the island, and hurled to their
deaths. At the height of the persecutions, the number of believers killed
on the Isle of Rocks never fell below ten per month, according to
contemporary reports. To simplify matters, the officers would sometimes bind several prisoners together in a rush mat and toss them into
the frigid seas. Virtually none of the bodies of these martyrs was ever
recovered.

I read over the grisly history of the island's martyrs until past noon.
The drizzling rain continued to fall.

At lunchtime the priest was nowhere to be seen. A sunburned,
middle-aged woman with jutting cheekbones served my meal. I judged
her to be the wife of some fisherman, but in the course of conversation I
learned to my surprise that she was a nun who had devoted herself to a
life of celibate service. The image I had always fostered of nuns was
limited to those women I often saw in Tokyo with their peculiar black
robes. This woman told me about the order of sisters in this area, known
in the local jargon as 'The Servants' Quarters'. The order, to which she
belonged, practised communal living, worked in the fields the same as
the other farm women, looked after children at the nursery school, and
tended the sick in the hospital.

'Father went on his motorcycle to Mount Fudō. He said he'd be back
around three o'clock.' Her eyes shifted towards the rain-splattered
window. 'With this awful weather, you must be terribly bored, Sensei.
Jirō from the office said he'd be by soon to show you the Christian
graves.'

Jirō was the young man with the bicycle who had been standing beside
the priest when I arrived the previous night.

Just as she predicted, Jirō appeared soon after I had finished lunch and invited me to accompany him. He even brought along a pair of boots for me to wear.

'I didn't think you'd want to get your shoes all muddy.'

He apologized that the boots were so old, bowing his head so incessantly that I was embarrassed.

'I'm ashamed to make you ride in a truck like this,' he added.

As we drove along the streets in his little van, I found that the mental picture I had drawn the previous night was accurate. All the houses were squat, and the village reeked of fish. At the dock, about ten small boats were preparing to go to sea. The only buildings made of reinforced concrete were the village office and the primary school. Even the 'main street' gave way to thatched-roofed farmhouses after less than five minutes. The telephone poles were plastered with rain-soaked advertisements for a strip show. They featured a picture of a nude woman cupping her breasts; the show bore the dreadful title 'The Sovereign of Sex'.

'Father is heading a campaign to stop these shows in the village.'

'But I'll bet the young men spend all their free time there. Even the young Christians . . .'

My attempt at humour fell on deaf ears as Jirō tightened his grip on the steering wheel. I quickly changed the subject.

'About how many Christians are there on the island now?'

'I think around a thousand.'

In the seventeenth century the number had been calculated at fifteen hundred, meaning a loss of about one-third since that time.

'And how many *kakure*?'

'I'm really not sure. I imagine they get fewer in number every year. Only the old people stick to their practices. The young ones say the whole thing's ridiculous.'

Jirō related an interesting story. In spite of frequent encouragement from the priests and believers, the *kakure* had refused to reconvert to Catholicism. They claimed that it was their brand of Christianity which had been handed down from their ancestors, making it the true original faith; they further insisted that the Catholicism brought back to Japan in the Meiji period was a reformed religion. Their suspicions were confirmed by the modern attire of the priests, which differed radically from that of the padres they had been told about over the generations.

'And so one French priest had a brilliant idea. He dressed up like one of the padres from those days and went to visit the *kakure*.'

'What happened?'

'The *kakure* admitted he looked a lot like the real thing, but something was wrong. They just couldn't believe him!'

I sensed a degree of contempt towards the *kakure* in Jirō's tale, but I laughed aloud anyway. Surely the French priest who went to all the trouble of dressing up like a friar from the seventeenth century had had a sense of humour about him. The story seemed somehow exhilaratingly typical of this island.

Once we left the village, the grey road extended out along the coast. Mountains pressed in from our left, the ocean to our right. The waters churned, a leaden colour, and when I rolled down the window an inch, a gust of rainy wind pelted my face.

Jirō stopped his truck in the shelter of a windbreak and held out an umbrella for me. The earth was sandy, dotted here and there with growths of tiny pine shrubs. The Christian graveyard lay at the crest of a sand-dune perched precariously over the ocean. It hardly deserved to be called a graveyard. The single stone marker was so tiny that even I could have lifted it with a little effort, and a good third of it was buried beneath the sand. The face of the stone was bleached grey by the wind and rain; all that I could make out was a cross that seemed to have been scratched into the rock with some object, and the Roman letters M and R. Those two characters suggested a name like 'Maria', and I wondered if the Christian buried here might have been a woman.

I had no idea why this solitary grave had been dug in a spot so far removed from the village. Perhaps some relative had quietly moved it to this inconspicuous location after the exterminations. Or possibly, during the persecution, this woman had been executed on this very beach.

A choppy sea stretched out beyond this forsaken Christian grave. The gusts pounding the windbreak sounded like electric wires chafing together. In the offing I could see a tiny black island, the Isle of Rocks where Christians from this district had been strung together like beads and hurled into the waters below.

I learned how to lie to my mother.

As I think back on it now, I suppose my lies must have sprung from some sort of complex I had about her. This woman, who had been driven to seek consolation in religion after being abandoned by her husband, had redirected the fervour she had once expended in search of the one true violin note towards a quest for the one true God. I can comprehend that zeal now, but as a child it suffocated me. The more she compelled me to share her faith, the more I fought her oppressive power, the way a drowning child struggles against the pressure of the water.

One of my friends at school was a boy called Tamura. His father ran a brothel at Nishinomiya.He always had a filthy bandage wound about his neck and he was often absent from school; I suppose he must have had tuberculosis even then. He had very few friends and was constantly mocked by the conscientious students. Certainly part of the reason I latched onto him was a desire to get back at my strict mother.

The first time I smoked a cigarette under Tamura's tutelage, I felt as though I was committing a horrid sin. Behind the archery range at school, Tamura, sensitive to every noise around us, stealthily pulled a crumpled cigarette pack from the pocket of his school uniform.

'You can't inhale deeply right at first. Try just a little puff at a time.'

I hacked, choked by the piercing smoke that filled my nose and throat. At that moment, my mother's face appeared before me. It was her face as she prayed with her rosary in the predawn darkness. I took a deeper drag on the cigarette to exorcize this vision.

Another thing I learned from Tamura was going to movies on my way home from school. I slipped into the darkened Niban Theatre near the Nishinomiya Hanshin Station, following Tamura like a criminal. The smell from the toilet filled the auditorium. Amid the sounds of crying babies and the coughs of old men, I listened to the monotonous gyrations of the movie projector. My whole mind was absorbed with thoughts of what my mother would be doing just then.

'Let's go home.'

Over and over I pressed Tamura to leave, until finally he snarled angrily, 'Stop pestering me! Go home by yourself, then!'

When we finally went outside, the Hanshin train that sped past us was carrying workers back to their homes.

'You've got to stop being so scared of your mother.' Tamura shrugged his shoulders derisively. 'Just make up a good excuse.'

After we parted, I walked along the deserted road, trying to think up a convincing lie. I hadn't come up with one until I stepped through the doorway.

'We had some extra classes today,' I caught my breath and blurted out. 'They said we have to start preparing for entrance exams.' When it was obvious that my mother had believed me, a pain clutched at my chest even as I experienced an inner feeling of satisfaction.

To be quite honest, I had no true religious faith whatsoever. Although

I attended church at my mother's insistence, I merely cupped my hands together and made as if to pray, while inwardly my mind roamed over empty landscapes. I recalled scenes from the many movies I seen with Tamura, and I even thought about the photographs of naked women he had shown me one day. Inside the chapel the faithful stood or knelt in response to the prayers of the priest reciting the Mass. The more I tried to restrain my fantasies, the more they flooded into my brain with mocking clarity.

I truly could not understand why my mother believed in such a religion. The words of the priest, the stories in the Bible, the crucifix – they all seemed like intangible happenings from a past that had nothing to do with us. I doubted the sincerity of the people who gathered there each Sunday to clasp their hands in prayer even as they scolded their children and cleared their throats. Sometimes I would regret such thoughts and feel apologetic towards my mother. And I prayed that, if there was a God, He would grant me a believing heart. But there was no reason to think that such a plea would change how I felt.

Finally I stopped going to morning Mass altogether. My excuse was that I had to study for my entrance exams. I felt not the slightest qualms when, after that, I lay in bed listening to my mother's footsteps as she set out alone for church each winter morning. By then she had already begun to complain of heart spasms. Eventually I stopped going to church even on Sundays, though out of consideration for my mother's feelings I left the house and then slipped away to pass my time wandering around the bustling shopping centre at Nishinomiya or staring at the advertisements in front of the movie theatres.

Around that time mother often had trouble breathing. Sometimes, just walking down the street, she would stop suddenly and clutch her chest, her face twisted into an ugly grimace. I ignored her. A sixteen-year-old boy could not imagine what it was to fear death. The attacks passed quickly, and she was back to normal within five minutes, so I assumed it was nothing serious. In reality, her many years of torment and weariness had worn out her heart. Even so, she still got up at five o'clock every morning and, dragging her heavy legs, walked to the station down the deserted road. The church was two stops away on the train.

One Saturday, unable to resist the temptation, I decided to play truant from school and got off the train near an amusement district. I left my school bag at a coffee shop that Tamura and I had begun to frequent. I still had quite a bit of time before the film started. In my pocket I carried a one-yen note I had taken from my mother's purse several days earlier. Somewhere along the way I had picked up the habit of dipping into her wallet. I sat through several movies until sunset, then returned home with a look of innocence on my face.

When I opened the door, I was surprised to see my mother standing there. She stared at me without saying a word. Then slowly her face contorted, and tears trickled down her twisted cheeks. It seems she had found out everything through a phone call from my school. She wept softly in the room adjoining mine until late into the night. I stuck my fingers in my ears, trying to block out the sound, but somehow it insinuated itself into my eardrums. Thoughts of a convenient lie to get me out of this situation left me little room for remorse.

Afterwards Jirō took me to the village office. While I was examining some local artefacts, sunlight began to warm the windows. I glanced up and saw that the rain had finally stopped.

'You can see a few more of these if you go over to the school.' Mr Nakamura, a deputy official in the village, stood beside me with a worried expression on his face, as though it were his personal responsibility that there was nothing here worth looking at. The only displays at the village office and the elementary school were of some earthenware fragments from remote antiquity, dug up by the teachers at the school. They had none of the *kakure* relics that I was eager to examine.

'Don't you have any *kakure* rosaries or crosses?'

Mr Nakamura shook his head with embarrassed regret. 'Those people like to keep things to themselves. You'll just have to go there yourself. They're a bunch of eccentrics, if you ask me.'

His words were filled with the same contempt for the *kakure* that I had detected in Jirō's remarks.

Jirō, having observed the weather conditions, returned to the village office and announced cheerfully, 'It's cleared up. We'll be able to go tomorrow for sure. Would you like to go and see the Isle of Rocks now?'

When we had visited the Christian grave, I had especially asked to see the Isle of Rocks.

Mr Nakamura made a quick phone call to the fishermen's union. Village offices can be useful at such times; the union was more than willing to provide us with a small motorboat.

I borrowed a mackintosh from Mr Nakamura. He accompanied Jirō and me to the dock, where a fisherman had the boat waiting. A mat had been laid in the wet bilges for us to sit on. In the murky waters that slopped around our feet floated the tiny silver body of a dead fish.

With a buzz from the motor, the boat set out into the still rough seas, vibrating ever more fiercely. It was invigorating to ride the crest of a wave, but each time we sank into a trough, I felt as though my stomach were cramping.

'The fishing's good at the Isle of Rocks,' Nakamura commented. 'We often go there on holidays. Do you fish, Sensei?'

When I shook my head, he gave me a disappointed look and began boasting to Jirō and the fisherman about the large silthead he had once caught.

The spray drenched my mackintosh. The chill of the sea winds rendered me speechless. The surface of the water, which had started out grey, was now a dark, cold-looking black. I thought of the Christians who had been hurled into these waters four centuries before. If I had been born in such a time, I would not have had the strength to endure such a punishment. Suddenly I thought of my mother. I saw myself strolling around the entertainment district at Nishinomiya, then telling lies to my mother.

The little island drew closer. True to its name, it was composed entirely of craggy rocks, the very crest of which was crowned with a scant growth of vegetation. In response to a question from me, Mr Nakamura reported that, aside from occasional visits by officials of the Ministry of Postal Services, the island was used by the villagers only as a place from which to fish.

Ten or so crows squawked hoarsely as they hovered over the top of the islet. Their calls pierced the wet grey sky, giving the scene an eerie, desolate air. Now we had a clear view of the cracks and fissures in the rocks. The waves beat against the crags with a roar, spewing up white spray.

I asked to see the spot from which the Christians were cast into the sea, but neither Jirō nor Nakamura knew where it was. Most likely there had not been one particular location; the faithful had probably been thrown down from any convenient place.

'It's frightening even to think about it.'

'It's impossible to imagine nowadays.'

Evidently the thoughts that had been running through my head had not even occurred to my two Catholic companions.

'There's lots of bats in these caves. When you get up close, you can hear them shrieking.'

'They're strange creatures. They fly so fast, and yet they never bump into anything. I hear they've got something like radar.'

'Well, Sensei, shall we take a walk around and then go back?'

The island from which we had come was being pounded by white surf. The rainclouds split open, and we had a clear view of the mountain slopes in the distance.

Mr Nakamura, pointing towards the mountains as the priest had done the previous evening, said, 'That's where the *kakure* village is.'

'Nowadays I suppose they don't keep to themselves like they used to, do they?'

'As a matter of fact, they do. We had one working as a janitor at the school. Shimomura was his name. He was from the *kakure* village. But I didn't much care for him. There wasn't anything to talk to him about.'

The two men explained that the Catholics on the island were hesitant about associating with the *kakure* or intermarrying with them. Their reluctance seemed to have more to do with psychological conflicts than with religious differences. Even now the *kakure* married their own kind; if they did otherwise, they would not be able to preserve their faith. This custom reinforced their conviction that they were a peculiar people.

On the breast of those mountains half concealed in mist, the *kakure* Christians had sustained their religious faith for three hundred years, guarding their secret institutions from outsiders, as was done in all the *kakure* villages, by appointing people to such special village posts as 'Waterworks Official', 'Watchman', 'Greeter' and 'Ombudsman'. From grandfather to father, and from father to son, their formal prayers were passed through the generations, and their objects of worship were concealed behind the dark Buddhist altars. My eyes searched the mountain slope for that isolated village, as though I were gazing at some forsaken landscape. But of course it was impossible to spot it from there.

'Sensei, why are you interested in such a strange group of people?' Nakamura asked me in amazement. My reply was noncommittal.

One clear autumn day, I bought some chrysanthemums and set out for the cemetery. My mother's grave is in a Catholic cemetery in Fuchū. I can't begin to count the number of times I have made the journey to that graveyard since my school-days. In the past, the road was surrounded by groves of chestnut and buckeye trees and fields of wheat; in the spring it was a pleasant path for a leisurely stroll. But now it is a busy thoroughfare crowded with all manner of shops. Even the stone carver's little hut that once stood all by itself at the entrance to the cemetery has turned into a solid one-storey building.

Memories flood my mind each time I visit that place. I went to pay my respects the day I graduated from the university. The day before I was due to board a ship for France to continue my studies, I again made the journey there. It was the first spot I visited when I fell ill and had to return to Japan. I was careful to visit the grave on the day I was married, and on the day I went into the hospital. Sometimes I make the pilgrimage without telling anyone, not even my wife. It is the spot where I conduct private conversations with my mother. In the depths of my heart lurks a desire not to be disturbed even by those who are close to me. I make my way down the path. A statue of the Holy Mother stands in the centre of the graveyard, surrounded by a tidy row of stone markers belonging to the graves of foreign nuns who have been buried here in Japan. Branching out from this centre point are white crosses and gravestones. A bright sun and a peaceful silence hover over each of the graves.

Mother's grave is small. My heart constricts whenever I look at that tiny grave marker. I pluck the wild grasses that surround it. With buzzing wings, insects swarm around me as I work in solitude. There is no other sound.

As I pour a ladle of water into the flower vase, I think (as I always do) of the day my mother died. The memory is a painful one for me. I was not with her when she collapsed in the hallway from a heart attack, nor was I beside her when she died. I was at Tamura's house, doing something that would have made her weep had she seen it.

Tamura had pulled a sheaf of postcards wrapped in newspaper from his desk drawer. And he smiled that thin smile he always wore when he was about to teach me something.

'These aren't like the phoney ones they sell around here.'

There were something like ten photographs inside the newspaper wrapping. Their edges were yellow and faded. The dark figure of a man was stretched out on top of the white body of a woman. She had a look as though of pain on her face. I caught my breath and flipped through the pictures one after another.

'Lecher! You've seen enough, haven't you?' Tamura cackled.

Their telephone rang, and after it was answered, we heard footsteps approaching. Hurriedly Tamura stuffed the photographs into his drawer. A woman's voice called my name.

'You must go home right away! Your mother's had an attack!'

'What's up?' Tamura asked.

'I don't know.' I was still glancing at the drawer. 'How did she know I was here?'

I was less concerned about her attack than the fact that she knew I was at Tamura's. She had forbidden me to go there after she found out that Tamura's father ran a whorehouse. It was not unusual for her to have to go to bed with heart palpitations, but if she took the white pills (I've forgotten the name) that the doctor gave her, the attack was always brought under control.

I made my way slowly along the back streets still warmed by the bright sun. Rusted scraps of metal were piled up in a field marked with a 'For Sale' sign. Beside the field was a small factory. I didn't know what they manufactured there, but a dull, heavy, pounding noise was repeated regularly inside the building. A man came riding towards me on a bicycle, but he stopped beside the dusty, weed-covered field and began to urinate.

My house came into view. The window to my room was half open, the way it always was. Neighbourhood children were playing in front of the house. Everything was normal, and there was no sign that anything unusual had happened. The priest from our church was standing at the front door. ·

'Your mother . . . died just a few moments ago.' He spoke each word softly and clearly. Even a mindless middle-school student like myself could tell that he was struggling to suppress the emotion in his voice. Even a mindless middle-school student like myself could sense the criticism in his voice.

In the back room, my mother's body was surrounded by neighbours and people from the church, sitting with stooped shoulders. No one turned to look at me; no one spoke a word to me. I knew from the stiffness of their backs that they all were condemning me.

Mother's face was white as milk. A shadow of pain still lingered between her brows. Her expression reminded me of the look on the face of the woman in the photographs I had just been examining. Only then did I realize what I had done, and I wept.

I finish pouring the water from the bucket and put the chrysanthemums into the vase that is part of the gravestone. The insects that have been buzzing about my face now cluster around the flowers. The earth beneath which my mother lies is the dark soil peculiar to the Musashi Plain. At some point I too will be buried here, and as in my youth, I will be living alone again with my mother.

I had not given Mr Nakamura a satisfactory answer when he asked me why I was interested in the *kakure*.

Public curiosity about the *kakure* has increased recently. This 'hidden' religion is an ideal subject for investigation by those doing research in comparative religion. NHK, the national educational channel, has done several features on the *kakure* of Gotō and Ikitsuki, and many of the foreign priests of my acquaintance come to visit the *kakure* whenever they are in Nagasaki. But I am interested in the *kakure* for only one reason – because they are the offspring of apostates. Like their ancestors, they cannot utterly abandon their faith; instead they live out their lives, consumed by remorse and dark guilt and shame.

I was first drawn to these descendants of apostates after I had written a novel set in the Christian era. Sometimes I catch a glimpse of myself in these *kakure*, people who have had to lead lives of duplicity, lying to the world and never revealing their true feelings to anyone. I too have a secret that I have never told anyone, and that I will carry within myself until the day I die.

That evening I drank *sake* with the Father, Jirō and Mr Nakamura. The nun who had served me lunch brought out a large tray stacked with raw sea urchins and abalone. The local *sake* was too sweet for someone like myself who drinks only the dry variety, but the sea urchins were so fresh they made the Nagasaki ones seem almost stale. The rain had let up earlier, but it began to pour again. Jirō got drunk and began to sing.

> Oh, let us go, let us go
> To the Temple of Paradise, let us go,
> Oh, oh.
>
> They call it the Temple of Paradise,
> They say it is spacious and grand.
> But whether it is large or small
> Is really up to my heart.

I knew the song. When I'd visited Hirado two years before, the Christians there had taught it to me. The melody was complicated and impossible to remember, but as I listened to Jirō's plaintive singing, I thought of the dark expressions on the faces of the *kakure*. Protruding cheekbones and sunken eyes that seemed to be fixed on a single point in space. Perhaps, as they waited through the long years of national isolation for the boats of the missionaries that might never return, they muttered this song to themselves.

'Mr Takaishi on Mount Fudō – his cow died. It was a good old cow.' The priest was unlike the man I had met at the party in Tokyo. With a cup or so of *sake* in him, he was flushed down to his neck as he spoke to Mr Nakamura. Over the course of the day, he and Jirō had perhaps ceased to regard me as an outsider. Gradually I warmed to this countrified priest, so unlike the swaggering prelates of Tokyo.

'Are there any *kakure* on Mount Fudō?' I asked.

'None. Everyone there belongs to our parish.' He thrust out his chest a bit as he spoke, and Jirō and Nakamura nodded solemnly. I had noticed that morning how these people seemed to look down upon the *kakure* and regard them with contempt.

'There's nothing we can do about them. They won't have anything to do with us. Those people behave like some kind of secret society.'

The *kakure* of Gotō and Ikitsuki were no longer as withdrawn as those on this island. Here even the Catholics appeared to be wary of the secretiveness of the *kakure*. But Jirō and Mr Nakamura had *kakure* among their ancestors. It was rather amusing that the two of them now seemed to be oblivious of that fact.

'What exactly do they worship?'

'What do they worship? Well, it's no longer true Christianity.' The priest sighed in consternation. 'It's a form of superstition.'

They gave me another interesting piece of information. The Catholics on the island celebrate Christmas and Easter according to the Western calendar, but the *kakure* secretly continue to observe the same festivals according to the old lunar calendar.

'Once when I went up the mountain, I found them all gathered together on the sly. Later I asked around and discovered they were celebrating their Easter.'

After Nakamura and Jirō left, I returned to my room. My head felt feverish, perhaps due to the *sake*, and I opened the window. The ocean was pounding like a drum. Darkness had spread thickly in all directions. It seemed to me that the drumming of the waves deepened the darkness and the silence. I have spent nights in many different places, but I have never known a night as fathomless as this.

I was moved beyond words as I reflected on the many long years that the *kakure* on this island would have listened to the sound of this ocean. They were the offspring of traitors who had abandoned their religious beliefs because of the fear of death and the infirmities of their flesh.

Scorned by the officials and by the Buddhist laity, the *kakure* had moved
to Gotō, to Ikitsuki, and here to this island. Nevertheless, they had been
unable to cast off the teachings of their ancestors, nor did they have the
courage to defend their faith boldly like the martyrs of old. They had
lived amid their shame ever since.

Over the years, that shame had shaped the unique features of their
faces. They were all the same – the four or five men who had ridden with
me on the ferry-boat, Jirō, and Mr Nakamura. Occasionally a look of
duplicity mingled with cowardice would dart across their faces.

Although there were minor differences between the *kakure* village
organizations on this island and those in the settlements on Gotō or
Ikitsuki, in each village the role of the priest was filled either by the
'Watchman' or the 'Village Elder'. The latter would teach the people the
essential prayers and important festival days. Baptism was administered
to newly-born infants by the 'Waterworks Official'. In some villages the
positions of 'Village Elder' and 'Waterworks Official' were assumed by
the same individual. In many instances these offices had been passed
down through the patriarchal line for many generations. On Ikitsuki I
had observed a case where units of organization had been established for
every five households.

In front of the officials, the *kakure* had of course pretended to be
practising Buddhists. They belonged to their own parish temples and
had their names recorded as Buddhist believers in the religious registry.
Like their ancestors, at certain times they were forced to trample on the
fumie in the presence of the authorities. On the days when they had
trodden on the sacred image, they returned to their villages filled with
remorse over their own cowardice and filthiness, and there they
scourged themselves with ropes woven of fibres, which they called
'*tempensha*'. The word originally meant 'whip', and was derived from
their misinterpretation of the Portuguese word for 'scourge'. I have seen
one of these '*tempensha*' at the home of a Tokyo scholar of the Christian
era. It was made from forty-six strands of rope, woven together, and did
in fact cause a considerable amount of pain when I struck my wrist with
it. The *kakure* had flogged their bodies with such whips.

Even this act of penitence did not assuage their guilt. The humiliation
and anxiety of a traitor does not simply evaporate. The relentless gaze of
their martyred comrades and the missionaries who had guided them
continued to torment them from afar. No matter how diligently they
tried, they could not be rid of those accusing eyes. Their prayers are
therefore unlike the awkwardly translated Catholic invocations of the

present day; rather they are filled with faltering expressions of grief and phrases imploring forgiveness. These prayers, uttered from the stammering mouths of illiterate *kakure*, all sprang from the midst of their humiliation. 'Santa Maria, Mother of God, be merciful to us sinners in the hour of death.' 'We beseech thee, as we weep and moan in this vale of tears. Intercede for us, and turn eyes filled with mercy upon us.'

As I listened to the thrashing of the sea in the darkness, I thought of the *kakure*, finished with their labours in the fields and their fishing upon the waters, muttering these prayers in their rasping voices. They could only pray that the mediation of the Holy Mother would bring forgiveness of their frailties. For to the *kakure*, God was a stern paternal figure, and as a child asks its mother to intercede with its father, the *kakure* prayed for the Virgin Mary to intervene on their behalf. Faith in Mary was particularly strong among the *kakure*, and I concluded that their weakness had also prompted them to worship a figure that was a composite of the Holy Mother and Kannon, the Buddhist Goddess of Mercy.

I could not sleep even after I crawled into bed. As I lay beneath the thin coverlet, I tried to sing the words of the song that Jirō had performed that evening, but I couldn't remember them.

I had a dream. It seemed that my operation was over and I had just been wheeled back to my room; I lay back on the bed like a dead man. A rubber tube connected to an oxygen tank was thrust into my nostril, and transfusion needles from the plasma bottles hung over my bed had been inserted into my right arm and leg. My consciousness should have been blurred, but I recognized the greyish shadow that clutched my hand. It was my mother, and she was alone with me in my hospital room. There were no doctors; not even my wife.

I saw my mother in other places, too. As I walked over a bridge at dusk, her face would sometimes appear suddenly in the gathering clouds overhead. Occasionally I would be in a bar, talking with the hostesses; when the conversation broke off and a sense of empty meaninglessness stole across my heart, I would feel my mother's presence beside me. As I bent over my work desk late in the night, I would abruptly sense her standing behind me. She seemed to be peering over my shoulder at the movements of my pen. I had strictly forbidden my children and even my wife to disturb me while I was working, but strangely it did not bother me to have my mother there. I felt no irritation whatsoever.

At such times, the figure of my mother that appeared to me was not the impassioned woman who had played her violin in search of the one perfect note. Nor was it the woman who had groped for her rosary each morning on the first Hankyū-line train, deserted except for the conductor. It was rather a figure of my mother with her hands joined in front of her, watching me from behind with a look of gentle sorrow in her eyes.

I must have built up that image of my mother within myself, the way a translucent pearl is gradually formed inside an oyster shell. For I have no concrete memory of ever seeing my mother look at me with that weary, plaintive expression.

I now know how that image came to be formed. I superimposed on her face that of a statue of 'Mater Dolorosa', the Holy Mother of Sorrows, which my mother used to own.

After my mother's death, people came to take away her kimonos and obis and other possessions one after another. They claimed to be sharing out mementoes of my mother, but to my young eyes, my aunts seemed to be going through the drawers of her dresser like shoppers rifling through goods in a department store. Yet they paid no attention to her most valued possessions – the old violin, the well-used prayer book she had kept for so many years, and the rosary with a string that was ready to break. And among the items my aunts had left behind was that cheap statue of the Holy Mother, the sort sold at every church.

Once my mother was dead, I took those few precious things with me in a box every time I moved from one lodging-house to another. Eventually the strings on the violin snapped and cracks formed in the wood. The cover was torn off her prayer book. And the statue of Mary was burned in an air raid in the winter of 1945.

The sky was a stunning blue the morning after the air raid. Charred ruins stretched from Yotsuya to Shinjuku, and all around the embers were still smouldering. I crouched down in the remains of my apartment building in Yotsuya and picked through the ashes with a stick, pulling out broken bowls and a dictionary that had only a few unburned pages remaining. Eventually I struck something hard. I reached into the still warm ashes with my hand and pulled out the broken upper half of that statue. The plaster was badly scorched, and the plain face was even uglier than before. Today, with the passage of time the facial features have grown vaguer. After I was married, my wife once dropped the statue. I repaired it with glue, with the result that the expression on the face is all the more indistinct.

When I went into hospital, I placed the statue in my room. After the first operation failed and I began my second year in hospital, I had reached the end of my rope both financially and emotionally. The doctors had all but given up hope for my recovery, and my income had dissolved to nothing.

At night, beneath the dim lights, I would often stare from my bed at the face of the Holy Mother. For some reason her face seemed sad, and she appeared to be returning my gaze. It was unlike any Western painting or sculpture of the Mother of God that I had ever seen. Its face was cracked from age and from the air raid, and it was missing its nose; where the face had once been, only sorrow remained. When I studied in France, I saw scores of statues and portraits of the 'Mater Dolorosa', but this memento of my mother had lost all traces of its origins. Only that sorrow lingered.

At some point I must have blended together the look on my mother's face and the expression on that statue. At times the face of the Holy Mother of Sorrows seemed to resemble my mother's face when she died. I still remember clearly how she looked laid out on top of her quilt, with that shadow of pain etched into her brow.

Only once did I ever tell my wife about my mother appearing to me. The one time I did say something, she gave some sort of reply, but a look of evident displeasure flickered on her face.

There was fog everywhere.

The squawking of crows could be heard in the mist, so we knew that the village was near at hand. With my reduced lung capacity, it was quite a struggle to make it all this way. The mountain path was very steep, but my greatest difficulty was that the boots which Jirō had lent me kept slipping in the sticky clay.

Even so, Mr Nakamura explained, we were having an easier time of it than in the old days. Back then – and we couldn't see it now because of the fog – there had been just one mountain path to the south, and it had taken half a day to reach the village. The resourceful *kakure* had deliberately chosen such a remote location for their village in order to avoid surveillance by the officials.

There were terraced fields on both sides of the path, and the black silhouettes of trees emerged from the fog. The shrieking of the crows grew louder. I remembered the flock of crows that had circled the summit of the Isle of Rocks on the previous day.

Mr Nakamura called out to a mother and child working in the fields.

The mother removed the towel that covered her face and bowed to him politely.

'Kawahara Kikuichi's house is just down this way, isn't it?' Nakamura asked. 'There's a Sensei from Tokyo here who'd like to talk to him.'

The woman's child gawked at me curiously until his mother scolded him, at which point he charged off into the field.

It had been Mr Nakamura's sensible suggestion that we bring along a bottle of *sake* from the village as a gift for Mr Kawahara. Jirō had carried it for me on our trek, but at this point I took it from him and followed the two men into the village. A radio was playing a popular song. Some of the houses had motorcycles parked in their sheds.

'All the young people want to get out of this place.'

'Do they come to town?'

'No, a lot of them go to work in Sasebo or Hirado. I suppose it's hard for them to find work on the island when they're known as children of the *kakure.*'

The crows were still following us along the road. They settled on the thatched roof of a house and cawed. It was as if they were warning the villagers of our arrival.

The house of Kawahara Kikuichi was somewhat larger than the others in the village, with a tiled roof and a giant camphor tree growing at the back. A single look at the house and it was obvious Kikuichi was the 'Village Elder', the individual who performed the role of priest in this community.

Leaving me outside, Mr Nakamura went into the house and negotiated with the family for a few minutes. The child we had seen in the field watched us from a distance, his hands thrust into trousers that had half fallen down. I glanced at him and realized that his bare feet were covered with mud. The crows squawked again.

I turned to Jirō. 'It looks as though he doesn't want to meet us.'

'Oh, no. With Mr Nakamura talking to him, everything will be just fine,' he reassured me.

Finally an agreement was reached. When I stepped inside the earthen entranceway, a woman was staring at me from the dark interior. I held out the bottle of *sake* and told her it was a small token of my gratitude, but there was no response.

Inside the house it was incredibly dark. The weather was partly to blame, but it was so dark I had the feeling it would be little different on a clear day. And there was a peculiar smell.

Kawahara Kikuichi was a man of about sixty. He never looked directly at me, but always kept his fearful eyes focused on some other spot in the room as he spoke. His replies were truncated, and he gave the impression that he wanted us to leave as soon as possible. Each time the conversation faltered, my eyes shifted to different corners of the room, to the stone mortar in the entranceway, to the straw matting, or to the sheaves of straw. I was searching for the characteristic staff that belonged to the 'Village Elder', and for the place where they had concealed their icons.

The Village Elder's staff was something only he was allowed to possess. When he went to perform baptisms, he carried a staff made of oak; to drive evil spirits from a home, he used a silverberry staff. His staff was never made from bamboo. Clearly these staffs were an imitation of the croziers carried by priests in the Christian age.

I searched carefully, but I was unable to locate either a staff or the closet where the icons were hidden away. Eventually I was able to hear the prayers handed down to Kikuichi from his ancestors, but the hesitant expressions of grief and the pleas for forgiveness were like every other *kakure* supplication I had heard.

'We beseech thee, as we weep and moan in this vale of tears.' As he intoned the melody, Kikuichi stared into space. 'Intercede for us, and turn eyes filled with mercy upon us.' Like the song Jirō had crooned the previous evening, this was just a string of clumsy phrases addressed as an appeal to someone.

'As we weep and moan in this vale of tears . . .' I repeated Kikuichi's words, trying to commit the tune to memory.

'We beseech thee . . .'

'We beseech thee.'

'. . . Turn eyes filled with mercy . . .'

'Turn eyes filled with mercy . . .'

In the back of my mind was an image of the *kakure* returning to their village one night each year after being forced to trample on the *fumie* and pay their respects at the Buddhist altars. Back in their darkened homes, they recited these words of prayer. 'Intercede for us, and turn eyes filled with mercy upon us. . . .'

The crows shrieked. For a few moments we were all silent, staring out at the thick mist that drifted past the veranda. A wind must have got up, for the milky fog swirled by more quickly than before.

'Could you perhaps show me your . . . your altar icons?' I stammered through my request, but Kikuichi's eyes remained fixed in another direction, and he gave no answer. The term 'altar icons' is not Christian jargon, of course, but refers more generally to the Buddhist deities which are worshipped in an inner room of the house. Among the *kakure*, however, the object to which they prayed was concealed in the most inconspicuous part of the house; to deceive the officials, they referred to these images as their 'altar icons'. Even today, when they have full freedom of worship, they do not like to show these images to non-believers. Many of them believe that they defile their hidden icons by displaying them to outsiders.

Mr Nakamura was somewhat firmer in his request. 'He's come all the way from Tokyo. Why don't you show them to him?'

Finally Kikuichi stood up.

We followed him through the entranceway. The eyes of the woman in the darkened room were riveted on our movements.

'Watch your head!' Jirō called out from behind as we entered the inner room. The door was so low we had to bend over in order to go in. The tiny room, darker than the entranceway, was filled with the musty smells of straw and potatoes. Straight ahead of us was a small Buddhist altar decorated with a candle. This was certainly a decoy. Kikuichi's eyes shifted to the left. Two pale blue curtains hung there, though I had not noticed them when we came through the door. Rice cakes and a white bottle of offertory wine had been placed on the altar stand. Kikuichi's wrinkled hand slowly drew aside the curtains. Gradually the sections of an ochre-coloured hanging scroll were revealed to us.

Behind us, Jirō sighed, 'It's just a picture.'

A drawing of the Holy Mother cradling the Christ child – no, it was a picture of a farm woman holding a nursing baby. The robes worn by the child were a pale indigo, while the mother's kimono was painted a murky yellow. It was clear from the inept brushwork and composition that the picture had been painted many years before by one of the local *kakure*. The farm woman's kimono was open, exposing her breast. Her obi was knotted at the front, adding to the impression that she was dressed in the rustic apparel of a worker in the fields. The face was like that of every woman on the island. It was the face of a woman who gives suckle to her child even as she ploughs the fields and mends the fishing-nets. I was suddenly reminded of the woman earlier who had removed the towel from her face and bowed to Mr Nakamura.

Jirō had a mocking smile on his face. Mr Nakamura was pretending to look serious, but I knew that inside he was laughing.

Still, for some time I could not take my eyes off that clumsily-drawn face. These people had joined their gnarled hands together and offered up supplications for forgiveness to this portrait of a mother. Within me there welled up the feeling that their intent had been identical to mine. Many long years ago, missionaries had crossed the seas to bring the teachings of God the Father to this land. But when the missionaries had been expelled and the churches demolished, the Japanese *kakure*, over the space of many years, stripped away all those parts of the religion that they could not embrace, and the teachings of God the Father were gradually replaced by a yearning after a Mother – a yearning which lies at the very heart of Japanese religion. I thought of my own mother. She stood again at my side, an ashen-coloured shadow. She was not playing the violin or clutching her rosary now. Her hands were joined in front of her, and she stood gazing at me with a touch of sorrow in her eyes.

The fog had started to dissipate when we left the village, and far in the distance we could see the dark ocean. The wind seemed to have stirred up the sea again. I could not see the Isle of Rocks. The mist was even thicker in the valley. From somewhere in the trees that rose up through the mist, crows cried out. 'In this vale of tears, intercede for us; and turn eyes filled with mercy upon us.' I hummed the melody of the prayer that I had just learned from Kikuichi. I muttered the supplication that the *kakure* continually intoned.

'How ridiculous! Sensei, it must have been a terrible disappointment to have them show you something so stupid.' As we left the village, Jirō apologized to me over and over, as though he were personally responsible for the whole thing. Mr Nakamura, who had picked up a tree branch along the way to use as a walking-stick, walked ahead of us in silence. His back was stiff. I couldn't imagine what he was thinking.

RETREATING FIGURES

In the past, whenever I had a sleepless night I would deliberately set some unintelligible book by my pillow and flip through its pages until drowsiness set in. But these days I have to put on my reading glasses just to see what is on the page, and it has become such a bother that I've given up the old habit.

In its place, I lie in the darkness and think about the past. When I close my eyes, the faces of people I had completely forgotten slowly float up one after another like bubbles in water. Half of them are already dead, and of those that are still alive, I have no idea where most of them are now, or what they are doing.

I muse over each of those faces until I fall asleep; and I realize how old I have become. At some point I will die. I wonder if someone on a sleepless night will think of me.

I recall the pale face of a middle-aged woman. Her frail shoulders were concealed beneath a stark-black short coat the day she came diffidently out onto the veranda at the hospital. I was out putting birdseed into a feeder for the myna bird I kept in one corner. She greeted me with considerable reserve.

'Have they set a date for your operation?'

I shook my head. 'The doctors don't seem to be able to make up their minds.'

It's been fifteen years now. I waited many months in that hospital for my third operation. And this woman stayed for a long while in the room next to mine. Each day seemed an eternity, but I never heard a single sound coming from her room, even though it was separated from mine by only a single wall.

The card on the door to her room had the name Horiguchi. I supposed she was a housewife from somewhere in the old, established downtown part of Tokyo. She had few visitors; once every week or two a man who seemed to belong downtown would drop in, dressed in an

unbecoming suit of Western clothes. He looked like the owner of an
electrical goods shop or a clothing wholesaler, and I assumed he was her
husband.

Even though we had lived next door to one another for over half a
year, she and I had never spoken. Our first conversation took place that
winter on the veranda where I was feeding the myna bird.

I was thoroughly drained from what was nearly a three-year stay in the
hospital and two major operations. I no longer had any hope that I would
recover, and I had ceased to believe in the specious words of consolation
dispensed by the doctors. Though I was grateful to those who came to
visit me, sometimes I was too weary even to want to talk to them. Such
feelings had prompted me to shell out a good deal of money to buy
myself a myna bird.

Late at night, when a hush had settled over the hospital, I would lie
alone in my room and talk to the bird. 'Will I die if I have another
operation?' The myna bird tilted its head and answered, 'Ye-es.' 'Is
there a God?' 'Ye-es.' I peered into its moist eyes. This bird is the only
one who will not lie to me, I decided.

'Is that a myna bird?' I heard a voice asking one day when I was out on
the veranda. I turned to see Mrs Horiguchi from the next room. The
winter sun that shone on her was feeble, and her face was drained of
colour. She looked at me, then at the bird-cage, and muttered as though
to herself, 'It's a good idea to roll the paste into a big ball and give it to the
bird when he's hungry.'

Then she was silent for a moment.

'About a year ago . . . I decided I wanted to get a bird that could talk as
we do. We're all very much the same, aren't we?'

We're all very much the same – from that single remark it was evident
that Mrs Horiguchi too had endured her illness for a long while. For
some reason I thought of the story in the Bible about the woman with an
issue of blood.

After that we conversed from time to time on the veranda. Even after
we got acquainted, it was a long while before I found out that she was
married to the famous Kabuki actor E. I had ignorantly assumed that the
well-dressed man who slipped in and out of her room was some sort of
shop-owner from downtown. And Mrs Horiguchi had seemed a bit too
plain and unassuming to be the wife of an actor who was so popular with
the young women.

'How long have you been ill?' I asked.

'Ten years.'

'Have you been in hospital all the time?'

'No. I go out, and come back in. I've been so much trouble to my husband.'

'I understand you're married to E., the Kabuki actor.'

'Yes. My husband is supposed to adopt a new stage name, but he's been putting it off and putting it off because of my illness.'

I didn't realize it at the time, but apparently when a Kabuki actor succeeds to the name of another performer, there are mountains of tasks his wife must undertake. Mrs Horiguchi explained that talk of her husband adopting a new name had started up two years earlier, but because her condition had worsened and she had gone back into hospital, her husband's supporter association had been forced to put off the ceremony.

'People are all very much the same.' I borrowed her phrase. 'I'm sure your husband would much rather have you completely well than have a new stage name.'

Her eyes lowered, Mrs Horiguchi said nothing. Her frail shoulders seemed smaller than they had before. I knew how meaningless my remark had been. I myself had stopped believing in the words of comfort spoken to me, and had started looking after a myna bird.

It was a long winter that year. One night when I lay back in bed staring at the ceiling, the lights suddenly went out. A patient on the third floor, unable to endure his suffering, had leaped from the roof and landed on top of the electric wires. I heard the sounds of nurses running down the corridor. They said he had broken his neck, but I felt no particular surprise. We were all very much the same.

'Well, let's see. We'll watch your progress for about three months, and then we'll decide whether or not to operate.'

A new year had dawned, but the doctor's words were as noncommittal as ever. In three months it would be spring. The cherry trees in the courtyard would be in bloom. But twice already I had seen those trees blossom from the window of this same room.

'With this particular illness . . .' The doctor took a pack of cigarettes from his pocket, but when he noticed my gaze, he grinned sheepishly and put it back. '. . . you should think of each year as being a month. That's still short compared to Mrs Horiguchi next door.'

'Is there any chance she'll recover?'

'She'll recover, all right. But she won't make it if she leaves the hospital again.'

In fact, several days earlier Mrs Horiguchi had come to consult me.

She could not make up her mind whether to leave the hospital or not.

'The question of a name change came up again at New Year's. I just don't feel right about making my husband and his supporters postpone it any longer.'

'Yes, but . . .' Aimlessly I repeated the words 'yes, but' over and over in my head. 'What do the doctors say?'

'The doctors? They always say the same thing. "Your chances of recovery have increased with this new medication, so you mustn't overdo things." '

She folded her arms and sighed deeply. She had tried virtually every drug available, and now had nothing to rely on but a newly-discovered antibiotic. If she left the hospital now and her condition deteriorated, there was little hope she would ever recover. I did not know what answer to give her. At our feet, the myna bird in his cage cocked his head and said something in a voice that sounded almost human.

I didn't see Mrs Horiguchi for a while after that. There was no sound from her room. It was as though the silence itself communicated her torment and anxiety. During the afternoon rest periods, I listened to the mute stillness of her room and waited for the decision she had to make. As I waited, I remembered what I had seen through the window of a room across the courtyard two years before, during the summer just after I entered the hospital.

The patient in that room had been a man in his fifties with leukemia. His young wife, always dressed in a white apron, had cared for him faithfully. Near the end of summer, I saw him wipe his mouth with a piece of paper and then stare fixedly at it. That was the day he realized that his gums were haemorrhaging. Once the gums haemorrhage, the leukemia has advanced beyond all hope of recovery.

Then, as now, I watched through the window each day, wondering what this man and wife would do. I know it was ill-mannered of me to spy on them, but I wanted to imprint a sharp image of human grief upon my eyes. And then one evening, with the setting sun blazing, I saw the two clinging to one another like little birds. They were seated on the bed, their eyes riveted on the floor. The husband who was about to die, and the wife who was about to be left behind, clutched one another's hands. I remembered that image as I listened to the utter silence coming from Mrs Horiguchi's room.

There was a heavy snowstorm in February. Even after the snow melted, a dingy layer of icy slush lingered in the courtyard. I caught a cold and developed a light fever. Each afternoon my temperature rose to about 100 degrees; from long experience I was able to judge my temperature without a thermometer merely by the flush in my cheeks and the languid weight of my limbs. I spent each day in bed looking at the myna bird, who cocked his head back at me.

One afternoon on such a day, there was a knock at my door. It was our rest period between one and three in the afternoon, so I knew it couldn't be a visitor. I opened my eyes and called, 'Who is it?' The door opened a crack, and Mrs Horiguchi's pallid face gingerly appeared.

'I want to thank you for everything you've done.' She was smartly dressed in a formal kimono and *haori* jacket. 'I've thought it over a great deal . . . and I've decided to leave the hospital.'

'Right now?'

'Yes.'

A smile flickered on her gaunt white face. The doctor's comment that she had little hope of recovery if she left now raced through my mind, but I said nothing.

'Thank you again.' She took a deep breath and said, 'You . . . be sure to take good care of yourself.'

The door closed softly. I climbed out of bed, hurriedly put on my slippers, and stuck my head out of the door. Mrs Horiguchi was walking away with her head bowed down the long, silent corridor. Her shoulders and back looked remarkably thin and small. Eventually I lost sight of her, but even after she was gone, the afterimage of her retreating figure remained before my eyes. Three years later I read in the obituary columns that she had died.

When my older brother moved to a new house, we came across an old photograph album. The thick cover had started to peel, and over the years the black cardboard on which the pictures were pasted had faded noticeably. I could remember most of the yellow-edged photographs, but there was a profile portrait of a woman with an old-fashioned hairdo whom I did not recognize, and three shots of a man with a moustache, wearing a suit. I could not remember ever seeing these pictures, and my brother knew nothing about them either.

In the photographs of my childhood, I am almost never smiling. I always have my eyes turned up in a rueful sort of glance.

'You always started blubbering whenever anyone tried to take a picture,' my brother laughed. 'You couldn't bear standing still.'

'Was I always that restless?'

'It's just the way you were as a child.'

As I flipped one by one through the discoloured photographs, I realized that in several places pictures had been deliberately torn out. The surface of the cardboard had been mercilessly ripped away in those spots.

'Why did these get torn out?'

'They were pictures of Uncle.'

'Uncle? Which uncle?'

'Uncle Kōzō, of course.'

My brother was very emphatic about the 'of course'. I felt a chill run through me and said nothing. The chill came from a revival of the feelings I had had towards this uncle for many years.

Uncle Kōzō was my father's youngest brother. For a long while – particularly during the war – he caused my family a good deal of consternation whenever anyone asked his whereabouts. In 1930 he fled from Japan and smuggled his way into the Soviet Union.

At night when I close my eyes, I can recall the outlines of his indecisive face. I don't know much about him as a person, but I do remember that face. As I think back on it now, I can't imagine how someone as weak-willed as my uncle mustered the courage in such a perilous age to join the student movement at Kyoto University under the very eyes of the police, and finally to escape from Niigata harbour to the USSR.

In the summer of 1929 I was in first grade at an elementary school in Dairen. The first report card I received during summer vacation was so indescribably bad compared to my brother's that I was thoroughly disheartened. Just after the beginning of the summer break, a tanned young man dressed in a splashed-pattern kimono appeared unexpectedly at our home, carrying an old trunk he had brought with him from Japan.

'This is Uncle Kōzō. You remember him, don't you?' my mother asked as I stood some distance away looking up at the young man. I shook my head, and my uncle smiled uncomfortably.

'This boy just barely met you before we moved here to Dairen,' Mother felt obliged to say. 'He's forgotten you.'

My mother even told my uncle how bad my grades had been. I'm sure she was just making idle conversation, but at the time I was deeply wounded.

During the summer vacation the local children came over to our house to play, but in the mornings we were all sent upstairs to do our studies. Sometimes my uncle, dressed in a light summer kimono, would be sent up to supervise us.

'Here he comes!' My sharp-eared brother would hear the footsteps on the stairs and whisper to us. The other children would scurry to their desks with innocent looks, but being the slow-moving sort myself, I was always the last to get back to my place. By the time my uncle came into the room, I would be standing alone on the *tatami* mats with a frightened look on my face.

'You've got to do your homework, you know,' he would say to me in exasperation.

Uncle tested me on my arithmetic, but frequently I was at a total loss.

'What's seven plus seven . . . ? Come on, look at your fingers. The answer's fourteen, isn't it?'

I gave him a look of stupid amazement and said nothing. I couldn't understand why it had to be fourteen rather than fifteen.

Unlike Father, however, our uncle never lost his temper or roared at us, and gradually we began to make fun of him. At the time, Mother had bought my older brother something called *The Riddle Book*, and he was engrossed in it. Relentlessly he would quiz Uncle Kōzō: 'What doesn't get full no matter how much you put in it?' or 'What never gets shorter no matter how much you cut it off?' Each time Uncle would shake his head, 'I don't know.'

My brother and I mocked him openly. 'Dummy! The thing that never gets shorter no matter how much you cut it off is water.'

At night, after we had finished supper, my father and uncle often talked together in the parlour for a long time. We children were busy setting off fireworks and had no idea what was going on, but father was admonishing his younger brother to give up the student movement. When the conversations ended, father would come out of the parlour with a look of obvious displeasure on his face. We looked up at them with apprehension, and Uncle would give us a taut, sheepish grin and disappear into his room.

It was a scorching summer. There was no humidity like in Japan, but even so a stifling heat hovered over the roads until nightfall. We played outside each evening until the leaves on the acacia trees had turned quite dark; the Manchurian children watched us with envy from a distance. Uncle Kōzō would sit by himself on a bench that he had set in front o the house, absorbed in his thoughts.

'What won't do what you want it to do unless you hit it on the head? My brother suddenly asked Uncle, bouncing a baseball off a wall. His train of thought interrupted, Uncle blinked his eyes and said, 'Now, what could it be?'

'A nail. A nail, of course! That's an easy one.' And with a brisk throw he hurled the ball against the dimly-lit wall. Uncle smiled forlornly. Then abruptly he asked:

'Well then, what grows shorter the longer it becomes?'

After some thought, my brother replied, 'Shadows on a summer day.' But my uncle shook his head.

About a week after that, Uncle Kōzō returned to Japan. Much later I found out that he had given much thought to whether he should leave the student movement, and he had apparently given my father his answer.

A horse-drawn carriage stopped in front of our house. With the end of his whip the Manchurian driver swatted at the flies that whirred around the horse's body. My brother and I tossed balls at the wall until our mother and father and uncle came out of the house. When he appeared at the doorway, Uncle was wearing the same splashed-pattern Kimono and carrying the same battered trunk that he had brought with him to Dairen.

'Well, goodbye,' he said. We said goodbye to him. He stroked my head and asked, 'Have you figured out what grows shorter the longer it becomes?' Then he climbed into the carriage with my parents. The driver cracked his whip, and the carriage slowly disappeared down the simmering road. The back of the splashed-pattern kimono grew smaller and smaller. That was the last I ever saw of my uncle.

Once he returned to Japan, he disappeared without a trace. Detectives went to my grandfather's house many times to investigate, but neither of my grandparents had any way of knowing where he was. The detectives told my grandfather that he had probably run away to China or the Soviet Union.

For a long while, this uncle was an annoyance to our family. Several times the police came to us to enquire about him. After my grandfather's death, only my grandmother was left to care about her son's welfare. Once she was gone, no one had any desire to find him.

The war was raging when I reached the same age my uncle had been when he came to Dairen. For some reason, whenever I heard the explosion of bombs dropped from enemy planes, I thought of my uncle's timid face. But I couldn't imagine why a man with so little courage would embrace a hazardous political philosophy and choose a perilous fate for himself. At the time, we could only think of Marxism as a dangerous system of thought. And the Soviet Union to which he had fled seemed like a nation of endless snowy climes. When I thought about him, I could almost hear him saying, 'What grows shorter the longer it becomes?'

The war ended. As more and more people were repatriated from Russia and China, my father apparently started making enquiries about my uncle's whereabouts, but he could find out nothing. Some two years after the termination of hostilities, a man suddenly appeared at my father's house. He was tanned by the sun, and his face looked very old for his age. When he placed his hands neatly on his knees, I noticed that he was missing half of a middle finger. He told us that he had been repatriated from the Soviet Union, and confided that he had fled Japan in company with Uncle Kōzō in 1930.

'At first we hid out in Sendai,' he began. 'But we couldn't stay there any longer, and we went to Niigata, thinking that we would escape to Russia. Kōzō pretended to be an artist, and made as though he was painting pictures at Niigata harbour. That was how we found out when the Soviet ship anchored there would be setting sail.'

Late one night when it appeared the ship was preparing to sail, this man and my uncle paddled a rowing-boat out into the murky sea and alongside the ship. They pulled themselves up a chain at the stern of the boat and climbed through a porthole leading into the cargo hold. A peculiar stench filled the darkened hold; they bumped into several objects that let out bizarre squeals. These turned out to be a herd of pigs that was being tended in the hold.

'Then the ship started to move. We spent the first night there with the swine. The crew got a jolt when we crawled up onto the deck the next morning!'

With a wry grin the man lightly related the circumstances of their escape. The two men were set to work scrubbing decks and were allowed to remain on the ship until it reached Vladivostock. There they were interrogated, and the Soviet authorities separated the two men, not allowing them to proceed to Moscow as they wished. This man had been sent to a town called Losolev, near Sakhalin.

'I don't know where they took Kōzō. I worked at a factory – that's where I lost half this finger in a machine – until the end of the war. After the war, I went to Sakhalin, did some work for the Japanese evacuees, and finally came back to Hokkaido.'

From him we learned that Uncle Kōzō had not returned to Japan, and that he was probably still somewhere in Russia. Or perhaps somewhere in that vast snow-bound country there was a tiny grave that belonged to him.

When I close my eyes in the dead of night, my uncle's timid face appears before me. And I can see again his retreating figure dressed in a splashed-pattern kimono the day he left Dairen in a horse-drawn carriage. My brother and I never could answer his riddle, 'What grows shorter the longer it becomes?' But now that I have reached my present age, I think the answer must be 'Life'. Something that grows shorter the longer it becomes – perhaps, as my uncle sat on that bench on a summer's evening in Dairen, he was thinking about the sort of life that is diminished the longer it becomes, and the kind of life that can seem long no matter how short. But it really makes no great difference. Now that I am over fifty, I am merely pained by the memory of his retreating figure.

With the air-conditioning on the blink, it was sultry in the basement bar. I was sitting on a corner stool drinking a beer when there were footsteps on the stairs, and a customer burst in, interrupting my reverie. He was about my age, and appeared to be an executive type.

'Quiet as a cemetery in here, isn't it?' he called. He seemed to be a regular; one of the two hostesses purred back, 'Well, after all, it is Saturday.'

'It's hot. Why'd you buy such a cheap cooler? It's because the mama-san's so stingy, isn't it?'

He plumped his stout bottom down on a stool a little way away from me, took off his glasses, and wiped his face vigorously with a hot towel.

'Just been golfing?' The bartender tried to humour the man.

'Are you kidding? I don't have time for that.'

I have trouble dealing with ebullient people like this one, so I turned my head away and listened to his overbearing voice.

'Isn't there any baseball on? There ought to be a game on TV.'

'I think it was probably cancelled with the late rain.'

'How can you be so sure? Turn on the TV. Come on, turn it on!'

Bottles of liquor were lined up in a row on a shelf that looked like a bookcase; in the corner was a tiny white television set. The bartender reluctantly flipped on the switch.

'The least you could do is buy a new television set.'

'I'm sorry. We don't use it much . . . See, it's been cancelled. They're showing a movie.'

On the screen, men on horseback and a herd of cattle were milling about on desert sands. It was just another Western.

'Damn. I came here to watch the game. Maybe I'll just go home.'

'Are you still a Hanshin fan?'

'You bet, and they're on a winning streak. Great, isn't it?'

From time to time the bartender gave me an apologetic look. I was supposed to meet someone here, but he hadn't shown up yet. The hostesses were watching the television, gloomy expressions on their faces. As though attracted to it by their interest, the noisy customer began to watch the screen.

A cavalry regiment was leading a wagon train across a broad grassy plain. At the edge of the plain a brown, skull-shaped mountain range came into view. I've never been to America, so I don't know what part of the country that scene represented. Suddenly the cavalry commander raised his hand and halted the procession. Spurring his horse, he rode up to one of the wagons and told the pioneers that he and his men would turn back here. The men and women in the wagon train waved their hands in farewell to the cavalrymen. The wagons gradually grew smaller and smaller as they advanced towards the edge of the plain. The scene changed to a commercial. For a moment it was silent in the bar.

'Good heavens.' One of the hostesses peered into the customer's face. 'You're crying.'

I looked over at him. He had removed his glasses and was rubbing his eyes with the palm of his hand.

'How very strange,' the hostess remarked.

With uncharacteristic bashfulness the man said, 'Scenes like that really affect me these days. . . . People riding off into the sunset.'

'But what's so sad about it?'

'You wouldn't understand.'

He laughed hoarsely and got up from his stool. As he climbed the stairs, I heard him teasing the hostess who had accompanied him in a deliberately jovial tone of voice.

I smiled at the bartender. 'He's getting to be about that age, isn't he?'

THE WAR GENERATION

Outside it was raining, and the restaurant was crowded. A steaming pot on a white charcoal brazier in front of them, office workers and various other customers blew on their onions and *kiritanpo** before eating them. A young woman dressed in a dark blue kimono with white splashes went from table to table setting down bottles of *sake*.

'Are these seats taken?' a businessman with a young woman in tow asked Konishi.

'No.' With his *sake* cup still at his lips, Konishi shook his head sourly. In truth he had wanted this table all to himself.

'Shall we have the fish broth?'

'Anything. I'm starving.'

She took a cigarette from her brown handbag and began to smoke. Looking at her, Konishi thought of his wife and daughters waiting for him at home. This woman would be about the same age as his oldest girl, but she brought the cigarette to her lips like a habitual smoker. It was a distressing sight.

'Don't you think they're charging a little too much for the year-end party this time?'

'What can we do? We have to go.'

Listening without interest to the whispered conversation between these two, Konishi concluded that they must work in the same section at some company. Their talk shifted from the cost of the year-end party to backbiting against their co-workers.

He consumed a good deal of time slowly drinking down his second bottle of *sake*. At home, his wife and daughters had probably already started dinner. He often stopped off for a few drinks on his way home from work, so his family would wait until seven o'clock and then go ahead and eat without him. Konishi felt more comfortable having them do that than making them wait for him.

As intoxication began to settle in, Konishi thought about the funeral

* A kind of rice pounded in a mortar, then steamed and eaten with chicken, etc.

of one of his fellow workers that he had attended the previous day. Mimura had been Personnel Director at the company, and was the same age as Konishi – fifty-two. He had heard that Mimura's blood pressure was a little high, but when the two of them had been tested together a year before in the company examination room, Konishi's blood pressure had been 150, Mimura's around 160. They had talked about how, by taking medicine, the pressure could be held below 200, and so there was nothing to worry about. But Mimura had died suddenly of a heart attack.

A photograph of Mimura, smiling and wearing a golfing hat, had been placed above the Buddhist memorial tablet surrounded by chrysanthemums. To one side sat the drooping figures of Mimura's wife, dressed in mourning kimono, and his son, wearing his high-school uniform. As he pressed his hands together reverently and gazed at Mimura's photograph, Konishi thought that this would be happening to him too before very long. Death, which had until now seemed still some distance away, had suddenly closed in on him with a whirr. In fact, two other funerals he had attended this year were for men in their fifties; he had to be on his guard.

'On my guard . . . ?' he muttered to himself. The woman who was sharing his table was putting fish and onions from the broth into a bowl for her date. The man, puffing on a cigarette, watched her as though he expected such treatment. Doubtless they had already slept together.

I must be on my guard. . . . But what was he supposed to do at this point? He was by no means satisfied with his job, but he had no intention of leaving. Eventually he would become an executive. Thereby he would avoid mandatory retirement. These days he had to feel very grateful for the position he was in. In his youth he had never imagined that his declining years would take their present shape. When he entered the Department of Law, he had planned to become a government official. Those plans had been aborted when he was taken out of school and sent off to war.

But Konishi had not been the only one that had happened to. All around him in those days were people who had had to change the direction of their lives because of the war. It was a matter of course for Konishi's generation.

He finished off his second bottle, and while he was debating whether to order a third, the glass door of the restaurant opened with a clatter. In the artificial light the rain looked like needles. A tall, thin woman in a black raincoat, around fifty or so, came into the restaurant.

Her nose was as pronounced as a foreigner's. Flecks of silver streaked her hair, like a foreigner's. Droplets of rain glimmered on her black raincoat. She asked the kimono-clad hostess a brief question and disappeared into a room at the back.

Still holding the empty *sake* bottle in his hand, Konishi let out an unintentional gasp. The man at the next table gave him a peculiar look.

None of the other customers in the restaurant knew who the woman was. But Konishi recognized the middle-aged woman as the violinist Ono Mari.

There was not a single clear sky over Tokyo in the days just before Konishi went into the army. Each day was leadenly overcast.

Though he knew it couldn't be the case, he wondered if the ashen skies over Tokyo had something to do with the city being as dark as his own feelings at the time. He had been at the university, and his boarding-house was located at Shinano-machi. Even the main road from there to Shinjuku was always deserted, every store had its glass doors tightly shut and displayed signs reading 'Closed'. Outside the shops, sandbags, buckets and fire blankets had been stacked in preparation for air raids. But there were no signs of human life.

Every day the sky looked as though it had been stuffed full of tattered cotton swabs. He could remember hearing sounds like faint explosions echoing constantly from the sky.

There was no longer anything resembling classes at the university. Instead, students like Konishi were sent to the F. Heavy Industries factory in Kawasaki, where they assembled airplane parts.

On the wintry mornings, factory workers and students dressed in work clothes and gaiters and carrying knapsacks over their shoulders lined up in single file on the square in front of Kawasaki Station. Buffeted by the cold wind, they waited and waited for their bus to come. Inside Konishi's knapsack he had some soya beans wrapped in paper, the only food that would help in some small way to stave off his hunger throughout the entire day.

Towards the end of 1944, the factory suffered a shortage of raw materials, and many machines ground to a halt. Even so, Konishi and the other grease-covered students had to stand in front of their drill presses all day long. Supervisors continued to make their rounds, marking down the names of any students whose work was slack. Those whose names were logged where not given any of the watery porridge that was brought around each day at three o'clock. Diluted as it was, the ravenous students coveted the porridge.

They were starved for more than just food. They likewise craved books. They yearned for heated rooms. They were hungry for human conversation, and for love. And so during the noon break, as they lined up in groups of five or six with their backs to the sunlit concrete wall, they discussed food and books. Then with sighs of longing they talked about certain members of the women's volunteer corps, who worked in a separate building. Dressed in their work pantaloons and wearing headbands, these woman sorted the various machine parts. Throughout the factory hung posters that read: 'Advance to Attu Island!'

As that year drew to a close, however, one after another of the young men who basked in that noonday sun received their draft notices printed on red paper. Each morning at the factory it was easy to tell from the looks on people's faces just who had received their orders. They would try to force a smile, but the dark, heavy circles under their eyes betrayed them.

'It's come,' the latest recipient would announce to everyone in a low voice, as though he were confessing some dark secret.

'When do you leave?'

'In two weeks.'

Of course, no one mouthed empty phrases like 'Congratulations' or 'Give it your best!' Sooner or later the same piece of paper would be coming their way. They all stared at the tall factory chimney. Again today the smoke from the chimney swirled straight up into the sombre sky. The scene was unchanged from yesterday or the day before. It seemed as though it would stay that way for eternity.

'When is this war going to end?' No one knew. They felt as though it would linger on and on for ever.

Whenever a new recruit left Tokyo, everyone assembled at Shinjuku or Tokyo Station to see him off. The students formed a circle on the crowded platform and sang their school song in an angry roar. They howled and leaped about, less interested in seeing off their friend than in masking the anxiety and fear that lurked in their own hearts. As the train carrying their comrade vanished from sight, looks of bleak emptiness appeared on the faces of those who had been so boisterous just a few moments before.

1945 came, and still Konishi had not received his induction notice. Around that time the enemy air raids gradually intensified. The previous November the Nakashima Aircraft Plant in Musashino had been bombed, and enemy planes appeared fifteen times the following month. Strangely, F. Factory in Kawasaki was untouched. Often the trains packed with exhausted workers at the end of the day would come to a stop with a groan. Sometimes there appeared to be an attack over the downtown area; from the train windows they could see the sky in that direction glowing a dark red. The train service was often suspended, and Konishi would have to crouch for a long while on a connecting platform at Tokyo Station, staring at the reddened sky, realizing with a start that death was all that lay before them.

On 28 February his good friend Inami received his draft notice, and the feeling that his own turn was coming soon struck Konishi with greater force than ever before. The night Inami's orders came, four or five of them gathered in his room for a farewell party. They drank rationed liquor and some watered-down medicinal alcohol they had stolen from the factory. Later that night, the landlord and the owner of an electrical shop who represented the local veterans' association came in and clumsily began to chant some Chinese poetry. 'Do your best! Work for your country.' They spouted callous words of encouragement. Inami, his face sallow, sat up straight in the student uniform he had not put on for some time.

That night he and Konishi slept in his room under the same blanket. Inami turned over, and Konishi could hear him weeping softly. He listened in silence for a while, then whispered, 'I'll be getting drafted too, before long.'

'Uh-huh,' Inami nodded. He turned so that Konishi could see the profile of his face. 'If you want anything of mine, you can have it.'

'I don't want any books. My red slip will be coming before I could finish reading any of them.'

'Probably. In that case, would you go to a concert in my place? I had to fight to get the ticket. I wanted to go to just one concert before the army got me.' He slipped out of bed in his worn-out underwear and rifled through his desk drawer until he found a brown-coloured ticket. Inami was engrossed in music: he had his own record collection, and even had a phonograph in his room.

'Whose concert?'

'Ono Mari on the violin. You've heard of her, haven't you – Ono Mari? They say she's a young genius.'

'I've heard the name a lot.'

In the dim light from the lamp swathed in a black cloth, Konishi looked at the brown ticket. On the coarse paper had been printed the words: 'Ono Mari Solo Violin Concert, March 10.' It hardly seemed possibly that a concert could be held in Tokyo now that death was everywhere.

'Are you sure I can have this?'

'Please go. In my place.'

Inami set out from Shinjuku Station the following morning. The usual clusters of students had gathered in circles on the platform to sing. Inami seemed thinner and shorter than the other students who were boarding the trains. He blinked his eyes behind glasses that kept sliding down his nose, and bowed his head repeatedly to his friends.

On the night of 9 March, a large formation of B-29s attacked Tokyo. The hour was approximately 12 a.m.

There was a strong northerly wind that night. A heavy snow had fallen in Tokyo two or three days earlier, and a thick layer of black ice still remained along the sides of the streets. Around six o'clock, Mari finished rehearsing for the following day's performance at the home of her accompanist, a White Russian named Sapholo, who lived nearby. She returned home, but because of the wind that had stirred up around noon, the long hair that was her trademark kept blowing across her face, and she had to stop many times along the way.

At the age of fourteen, she had left all the older violinists in the dust and taken first place in a music competition sponsored by the Mainichi Newspaper Corporation. Thereafter she attracted many fans. As a young child she had been in poor health, and the rowdy children at elementary school had made fun of her. Unable to endure the atmosphere, she had pleaded with her parents not to make her continue in school; they had agreed to let her pursue her violin and other essential studies at home. Perhaps that was why she was fawned upon there.

That evening, as she warmed her legs under the *kotatsu* and ate the potato pie and unsweetened black tea her mother had prepared for her, she discussed with her parents the possibility of going to Manchuria. The Musicians' Patriotic Society had proposed a series of concerts in Manchuria, and if possible she wanted her mother to go with her. Her father, wearing a frayed dressing-gown, agreed that they should go for about half a year, treating it as a kind of evacuation; there would be no air raids in Manchuria, and they would probably not have to contend with food shortages.

'This war should be over within half a year anyway.' Her artist father, who had studied in France as a young man, hated the military. He took an active part in air-raid drills and went to pay his respects to departing soldiers, but at the dinner table he often shared his grim outlook on the war situation with his wife and daughter.

Mari eventually grew tired and put her hand to her mouth to yawn. The radio had been playing a song called 'Look, a Parachute!', but suddenly it was interrupted by a shrill buzzer, and the announcer began to read a report from the Eastern Military Command.

'Enemy planes have been sighted over the ocean south of the city. They are approaching the mainland.' The announcer repeated the words three times.

'It's all right,' Mari's mother said. 'They're probably just reconnaissance planes.'

'Why don't we just go to bed instead of putting out the lights,' her father replied, extinguishing the coals in the *kotatsu*. 'I'm not about to do everything the army wants us to do.'

Mari fell asleep in her upstairs room. She had placed her violin case, air-raid hood and knapsack by her pillow, ready for an emergency, and had then dropped off to sleep as swiftly as a shower of falling pebbles. Soon in her dreams the orchestra members began to tune their instruments. The reverberations from the instruments were jumbled and confused, and somehow refused to modulate together as they usually did. Someone was beating on the kettledrum.

'Wake up! Mari, wake up!'

Someone was shouting at her bedside. She opened her eyes and dimly saw her father standing there wearing a metal helmet. Her ears still rang with the discordant strains of the orchestra.

'We've got to get away. It's an air raid! The flames are coming closer to us!'

For some reason her father's voice seemed to come from far away. She felt no sense of urgency at the words 'air raid.' Like a marionette she did as she was instructed and stumbled out of bed. It was then that she realized the noises in her ears were not those of an orchestra tuning up, but the crackling of fires somewhere nearby.

They joined her mother at the foot of the stairs and started for the air-raid shelter in the garden. As they hurried along, they looked up and saw that the sky over Honjo and Fukagawa was a flaming red. There was a popping sound like roasting beans, and they could hear the shouting, clamouring voices of many people. When they reached the shelter, their noses were stung by the smells of straw and damp earth.

'We can't stay here. We've got to run!' her father shouted. To her mother, who was carrying a rucksack and her purse, he called, 'Leave that. You don't need it.' Carrying just one rucksack on his back, he hurried the two women out through the gate. From the neighbouring Yoshimura house came clattering noises of others preparing to flee; on a road nearby a child cried, 'Ma-a-ama!'

The main street was already a maelstrom of people. The sky behind them was a sombre red. In the torrent were a man pulling his belongings along in a bicycle trailer, a young man carrying bedding in a hand-cart and a woman with a blanket wrapped around her body. All of them streamed towards the west, as though drawn by some phantom power. Time and again Mari's father shouted, 'Stay together!' Mari realized that the only thing she was carrying was her violin case. Another explosion shook the sky. The white bodies of the B-29s, their arms outstretched, appeared in the searchlights. The anti-aircraft guns opened fire, but the B-29s continued to soar calmly overhead. The wind still blew fiercely. From the distance echoed a succession of thunderous noises, as though a pile-driver were pounding the ground.

At his Shinano-machi boarding-house, Konishi was unable to get to sleep until about 2 a.m., thanks to the searchlights that glanced off his window and the explosion of anti-aircraft guns in the distance. The next morning he learned from the Imperial Headquarters bulletin that part of the city had been indiscriminately bombed by a hundred and thirty B-29s. The information bureau of the Headquarters and the newspapers reported without comment that fifty of the enemy planes had been damaged and fifteen shot down. But that day as he set out for the factory on the sporadically paralysed train line, Konishi saw that nearly all of the downtown sector had been consumed by fire in the previous night's raid. At the plant, workers gathered in small groups here and there, talking in subdued voices. Many of the labourers they were used to seeing had not shown up for work. From the student work-force, Taguchi, Ueno and Fujimoto were absent. A supervisor appeared and roared at the group, 'Get back to work!'

The ticket he had received from Inami was still carefully tucked into his train pass holder, but as he worked, Konishi began to have doubts that the concert would be held under the present circumstances. Besides, even if he tried to go to the concert, and there was another air raid like the one the night before, he would not be able to get back to his boarding-house. He decided it would be better not to go. When he reached that conclusion, though, he could hear Inami's plaintive voice echoing in his ears: 'I had to fight to get the ticket. Please go in my place.' He began to feel that wasting the brown ticket would be akin to betraying his friend. Without even asking, Konishi knew full well what sort of trials Inami was now enduring in the army.

At five o'clock the long, heavy siren announcing the end of the working day blared out. Still uncertain whether or not to go to the concert, Konishi crowded into the bus for Kawasaki Station with the other workers, then transferred to the equally packed train. Those who had found seats and those who dangled from the straps all had their eyes closed, and their faces looked as if they belonged to overworked beasts of burden.

It was pitch black at the deserted Yūraku-chō Station when Konishi got off the train and started walking towards Hibiya Public Hall. Along the way he took some of the paper-wrapped soya beans from his knapsack and chewed them. At the end of the day's labours his legs felt heavy and his stomach empty. When the dark hall at last came into view, he had to sit down on a rock in the park and rest for a while. Then he stood up and walked to the steps of the hall, where about fifty people had gathered by the entrance. Each of them wore gaiters and work pants and carried a knapsack on his shoulders.

As it was nearly six o'clock and the doors still hadn't been opened, someone asked his neighbour in the queue, 'Is there going to be a concert or not?' Word of mouth had it that the fires caused by the previous night's air raid had driven both Mari and her accompanist Sapholo from their homes; their whereabouts were unknown, and the hall was presently attempting to contact them. Still no one made a move to leave; they all stood patiently at the entrance.

Two men with stern faces, dressed in patriotic uniforms, appeared and bellowed, 'Hmph, what are you doing listening to enemy music in times like these? Go home, all of you!' The group lowered their eyes and said nothing. The men shrugged their shoulders and disappeared.

Before long a timid, middle-aged employee came out of the hall and announced apologetically, 'We have not been able to make contact. The concert is cancelled. I'm very sorry.'

No one protested. With shadows of resignation flickering on their backs, they silently began to disperse. Feeling somehow relieved, Konishi started to follow them out of the park. Just then a man at the front of the procession called, 'She's here!'

Everyone stopped walking. A weary, long-haired girl dressed in men's trousers and carrying a violin case was walking towards the hall with a look of pain on her face. It was Ono Mari.

'There's going to be a concert!' The shout passed from one person to the next like the baton in a relay race. The music enthusiasts turned on their heels like a flock of ducks and went back to the hall.

It was a peculiar concert, the sort not likely to have been seen before or since. The audience filled only half of Hibiya Public Hall, so the patrons dressed in their working clothes picked out seats to their liking and waited eagerly for Ono Mari to make her appearance.

Soon Mari came out onto the dusty stage, clutching her violin and bow in one hand. She had not had time to adjust her make-up, and the pained expression lingered as she stood in the centre of the stage. Exhaustion was etched into her face, and the renowned long hair and the wide, almost European eyes seemed agonizingly incongruous with the tattered men's trousers she was wearing. But no one laughed.

'We were burned out of our house,' she apologized, the violin and bow dangling from her hands. 'The trains couldn't go any further than Yotsuya . . . I walked here from Yotsuya. I had to come . . . knowing this might be my last concert.'

She bit her lip, and the audience knew she was choking down her emotions. There was not even a suggestion of applause. Everyone remained silent, pondering what she had just said.

At that moment, Konishi thought, 'This just might be the last concert I'll ever hear.'

Mari shook her head vigorously to get the hair out of her face, tucked the violin under her chin, leaned forward, bent her slender wrist sharply, and adjusted her bow.

From beneath that wrist the strains of Fauré's *Elegy* began to pour out. Not a single cough came from the audience. The tired, begrimed patrons closed their eyes and listened to the music, absorbed in their own private thoughts and individual griefs. The dark, low melody pierced the hearts of each one. As he followed the music, Konishi thought about the dying city of Tokyo. He thought of the scorched, reddish sky he had seen from the station platform. He thought of the drafted workers and students waiting in the chill winter wind for a bus to pick them up at Kawasaki Station. He remembered the thin face of Inami, the tear-stained face he had buried in his bedcovers the night before his induction. Perhaps the air-raid sirens would whine again tonight, and many more people would die. Tomorrow morning Konishi, the other members of the audience and Ono Mari might be reduced to charred grey corpses. Even if he did not die today, before long he would be carted off to the battlefield. When that happened, only the strains of this melody would remain to reach the ears of those who survived.

When she finished the *Elegy*, Mari played Fauré's *Après un rêve*, then performed the Saint-Saëns 'Rondo Capriccioso' and Beethoven's 'Romance'. No one even considered the possibility that at any moment the alarms might sound, that the sky might be filled with a deafening roar, and that bombs might start to fall with a screeching howl.

Something sticky brushed against his head. A spider had woven its web in the *yatsude* plants in front of his house. Konishi clicked his tongue and opened the glass door.

From the parlour he could hear music playing on the television. As a man in his fifties, he could not begin to comprehend the electric guitar music that so delighted his daughters. It sounded to him like nothing more than someone banging noisily on metal buckets.

He was balancing himself with one hand on the shoe cabinet and removing his shoes when his wife came out of the parlour. 'Welcome home,' she said, and a moment later his second daughter, a high-school girl, appeared and begrudgingly repeated the greeting.

'Clean up the entranceway. How many times do I have to tell you?'

His wife and daughter said nothing. With a sour expression he washed his hands in the bathroom and then gargled, making a sound exactly like a duck. When he had changed his clothes he went into the parlour. The two daughters who had been watching television got abruptly to their feet, looked at him coldy, and muttering, 'We've got homework to do,' headed for their rooms. Konishi cast a disappointed glance after them.

Konishi's wife chattered as she filled his rice bowl, 'Remember I told you that the owner of the Azusa-ya was complaining of stiff shoulders?' The Azusa-ya was a grocery store by the bus stop. 'He's gone into hospital. His wife says he's got some kind of growth in his chest. It looks like cancer.'

The shop-owner was not much older than Konishi. Once again he felt death closing in on him with a whirring sound. He remembered the funeral of Mimura, his co-worker who had died of a heart attack. No, death was not closing in on them. Since their schooldays, death had always lived alongside the members of his generation. That smouldering red sky he had seen from the platform at Tokyo Station. The buzz of enemy planes that constantly filled the clogged grey skies. Inami had died of an illness on the battlefield in Korea. Other friends had been killed in the South Seas or on islands in the Pacific. Somewhere within, he felt as though the postwar period was just an extension of life that he had been granted.

'Toshiko wants to go on a vacation to Guam with some of her friends.' Glumly he continued to eat while his wife went on talking. Her face was fleshy around the eyelids and chin. It occurred to him that when he had seen Ono Mari in the restaurant tonight, her hair was streaked with flecks of silver.

'I saw Ono Mari today,' he said, almost to himself.

'Who's she?' His wife smothered a yawn.

OLD FRIENDS

I had just returned from a wintry Poland and was still recovering from jet lag when I received an unexpected phone call from an old friend.

He was parish priest at a tiny church in Mikage, between Osaka and Kobe. Though he was three years younger than me, there was scarcely a hair left on his head. Come to think of it, when we were children, his father had shown up at church each Sunday with a shiny pate, too.

'Shū-chan!' He called me by the same familiar name he had used forty years before, when we had played catch together in the churchyard where red oleanders blossomed. I thought of his hairless head, and I found it amusing that this bald, fiftyish man was still squawking out 'Shū-chan!'

'Shū-chan, I know you're awfully busy. But do you think you could come out here next Sunday? To tell the truth . . .'

To tell the truth, he was calling because it was going to be the twenty-fifth anniversary of his investiture as a priest. He wanted to have a little get-together with some of his old friends, and wondered if I could come.

'Who's going to be there?'

'Akira-san, and Koike Yat-chan, and Eitarō.'

One after another he listed the names of friends I had not seen for many, many years. Ah, are they still alive? I mused. It was like standing on a hill at nightfall and looking down at a river twisting its way across a plain.

'Can you come?'

'Yes. I'll arrange it one way or another.'

No matter how much trouble it took, I had to go for the sake of my old friend. If I missed this opportunity, I might never see him again. We had reached that age.

I booked reservations on a Saturday-afternoon flight. Into my tiny flight bag I stuffed the first book I came across on my shelf – a paperback collection of poems by Itō Shizuo.

Above the path the moorhen travels
There is no need for a fragrant morning breeze,
No need for lacy clouds

I opened the book on the packed airplane and read these opening lines. Slowly, placidly, I tasted the verses with my tongue. They were delicious.

The rays of the sun had grown faint when I arrived at Itami Airport. My old friend had come to meet me, bringing along a student in tow. He clutched his beret in his hand and said, 'Thank you for coming.'

His hairline had receded even further than when I had last seen him several years before, and drops of perspiration glistened on his scalp. I tried to remember what he had looked like as a child, but for the life of me I couldn't summon up an image of his face. I recalled that he had been a clumsy child and a poor catcher when we played ball, but life had utterly wiped away all other traces of his youth.

We were riding along the highway towards Kobe in a Corolla driven by the student when my old friend suddenly remembered something and said, 'Say, listen. Father Bosch says he's going to come too.'

'Father Bosch?'

'I'll bet you're eager to see him, Shū-chan. He was always giving you the devil, wasn't he?'

I was glad I had come. I hadn't seen Father Bosch for over thirty years. Just after the war ended, this French priest had been released from the concentration camp in Takatsuki, but I was already living in Tokyo by then.

What my old friend said was true. As a child, I had often been scolded by the French cleric, who was in his forties at the time and sported a beard. Once when we were playing baseball in the church courtyard, a ball I had hurled smashed a window in his rectory. He appeared with a red face like that of Chung K'uei the demon-killer and dragged me off by my ear. When my dog came bounding into the chapel in the middle of Mass and startled the congregation, he roared that I was not to come to church any more.

'It's been so long. How old is he now?'

'Seventy-two. His health has deteriorated a bit, so he's been recuperating at the monastery in Nigawa. But he's going to come.'

'He's in bad health? What's the problem?'

'It's not any particular disease, but you know he was pretty badly treated by the MPs during the war. I suppose that's resurfaced now that he's getting along in years.'

The highway we were racing along looked nothing like I remembered it. The tracks of the railway I had taken to school as a child had been torn out and replaced by a strip of scruffy bushes. The black-shingled houses that had lined both sides of the road were transformed into bowling alleys and service stations that basked in the afternoon sun.

I could still remember the day Father Bosch was taken away by the military police. I did not see it happen. I had just returned home from middle school, and two or three Catholic housewives were there, telling my mother all the horrifying details. Plainclothes police and MPs had stormed into the rectory without taking off their shoes, rifled through every drawer in the place, and then taken the Father away. The housewives chattered timorously among themselves, unable to believe the accusation that the priest was a spy.

In those days every foreigner was suspect. The police and the military authorities kept an even closer watch on Catholic priests. Later we learned that Father Bosch had been arrested because of a camera and a photo album that he owned. They had come across a photograph of an airplane factory in his album.

From that day, Mass was no longer celebrated at the church. Even so, I heard that plainclothes detectives still came to survey the place from time to time. Rumours circulated that Father Bosch was being treated brutally by the military police. But we knew nothing of what was really going on.

The church in my old friend's parish at Mikage was hardly an imposing structure. On a plot of land barely sixteen hundred square metres stood the tiny church, the wooden rectory and a nursery school. While he made some phone calls, I watched absently as some children tossed a ball back and forth in the school playground.

One bespectacled boy was having trouble catching the balls flung at him by a chubby little fellow. His awkwardness made me think of my own youth. It had taken me until I was this old to realize that, at some time or other in their lives, people all taste the same sorrows and trials. Who could say that this boy was not experiencing the same grief I had felt forty years before?

My friend finished his work and came in to say, 'Everyone should be arriving between 5.40 and six o'clock. Do you want to wait here, or would you rather go into the chapel?'

To mark his anniversary, he was planning to celebrate Mass at six o'clock for his childhood friends who had been good enough to attend.

I entered the chapel alone and sat down. Two kerosene stoves had been placed in the aisle separating the men's pews from the women's; their blue flames flickered, but the chapel was still icy cold.

While I waited for the others to arrive, I thought about Father Bosch. It was now some thirty years since the end of the war, but he had remained here in Japan, labouring in the churches at Akashi and Kakogawa. He never thought of abandoning the people who had inflicted such cruel tortures upon him. Undoubtedly one day his bones would be laid to rest in this land.

These thoughts were prompted by the experiences I had had in Poland just two weeks earlier. A powdery snow had swirled through the sky over Warsaw each day, and at dusk a grey mist had enveloped the round domes of the churches and the squares gloomily overlooking the gates at the triumphal arch. People wearing fur caps shivered as they walked like livestock past the denuded trees in the squares. That dark, desolate vista had reminded me of the war, and in truth the scars of war were in evidence everywhere in that country. While I was in Poland I met a number of men and women who had survived the living hells at Auschwitz and Dachau. They rarely touched on their memories of those days, but there was one woman who rolled back the sleeve of her dress and showed me the convict number tattooed on her arm. 'This is what it was like,' she muttered sadly. The four digits clung to her slender forearm like ink stains. 'Now perhaps you will understand.'

As a child, she told me, she had spent a year in the Auschwitz camp. With the innocent eyes of youth she had looked on day after day as scores of her fellow prisoners were beaten, kicked, lynched, and slaughtered in the gas chambers.

'I am a Catholic, and I know I am supposed to forgive others . . . But I have no desire to forgive them.'

Her eyes were riveted on mine as she spoke. Her breath reeked of onions.

'Never?'

'I doubt if I will ever forgive them.'

Her despairing sigh echoed in my ears throughout my stay in Poland.

As I rubbed my hands together and waited in the unyielding pew for my old friend to celebrate the six o'clock Mass, I heard those words ringing in my ears once again. I could even smell the onions that fouled her breath.

Who is to say that Father Bosch doesn't feel the same way? I thought. Perhaps within the very depths of his heart there is one ineffaceable spot that will never be able to forgive the Japanese who flogged and trampled and tortured him.

Behind me the door to the chapel squeaked open. The sound of hesitant footsteps followed. I turned and saw three men standing with their overcoats over their arms. I had not seen them for many years, but I knew at a glance that they were Akira-san, Koike Yat-chan, and Eitarō. Layers of life and labour and age had piled up like dust on their youthful faces, too. Yat-chan saw me, raised a hand in greeting, and pointed me out to his companions. We merely exchanged glances; then they seated themselves in the cold chapel, where we maintained a respectful silence.

Our old friend appeared, dressed in his Mass vestments and reverently carrying the chalice swathed in a white cloth. At the altar decorated with two lighted candles, he began to intone the Mass. The chapel was silent, with just four of us in attendance, and the only other sound was an occasional cough from Akira-san.

Half-way through the Mass, where normally on the Sabbath he would deliver a sermon, our old friend blessed us with the sign of the cross and said:

'Thank you all very much. It is a great joy for me to be able to celebrate Mass for friends who once played in the same churchyard with me. Now twenty-five years have passed since I became a priest.' His salutation was spoken in standard Tokyo speech laced with a bit of the Osaka dialect.

'I am the only one of our group who joined the priesthood, but I have continued to pray for the welfare of each one of you.'

There were footsteps at the rear of the chapel; slowly, quietly they made their way forward, determined not to interrupt the priest's remarks. From the sound I visualized a bent old man. Father Bosch slipped into a seat at the front of the chapel and brought his palms together. His short-cropped hair was virtually white, and the shadows of physical debilitation and the loneliness of life were etched on his slender back. As I looked at his back, it occurred to me that shortly this priest would die here in Japan.

Sushi was served in the rectory dining-room. We clustered around Father Bosch, drinking beer and watered-down whisky. Both Yat-chan, now the manager of an auto-parts factory, and Akira-san, a pharmacist, were flushed red with liquor, and they related one tale after another from their youthful days.

'Father. Shū-chan was really rotten, wasn't he?' Yat-chan called to Father Bosch. 'Do you remember when he shinnied up the church steeple and pissed from up there?'

'Yes, I remember.' He smiled in my direction and said, 'I did have to reprimand you a lot.'

'I was scared to death of you, Father.'

'I would have had a mess on my hands if I'd let you go unchastened. As it was, I received a lot of complaints from the Women's Society. I really would have been in trouble if I hadn't scolded you.'

'Shū-chan was definitely on the black list with those old ladies of the Women's Society. We never thought he'd turn out to be a novelist.'

'I'm sure you didn't,' I grinned sardonically. 'I never dreamed I'd end up this way, either.'

Father Bosch took only a sip or two of beer and swallowed down a few pieces of sushi. He had lived in Japan for many years, but there was still a trace of awkwardness in the way he used his chopsticks.

The kerosene stove warmed the room with a soft, tranquil blue flame. From the depths of my memory, the faces of each of the parishioners who had once come to church on Sundays, at Easter, and at Christmas, floated up. These were faces I had forgotten for a long while.

As I drank down my umpteenth glass of diluted whisky, I remarked, 'There was that university student named Komaki – do you remember? What's he doing these days? He used to play with us sometimes.'

'Didn't you hear?' my old friend responded. 'He was killed in the war.'

I had heard nothing about it, since I had moved to Tokyo just after the defeat.

'Yamazaki and Kurita's father were killed too.'

'I knew about them.'

'The war was a terrible time,' Yat-chan muttered, staring at the rim of his glass. 'Just because we were Christians, they called us traitors and enemies at school and threw stones at us to torment us.'

There was silence for a moment.

Then suddenly everyone's eyes turned towards Father Bosch. We had indeed been persecuted, but he alone had been subjected to torture.

For just an instant, a look of confusion and embarrassment flashed across his face. Then he forced a smile for our benefit. To me it looked like a smile filled with pain. I thought of the oniony breath of the Polish woman when she had said, 'I doubt if I will ever forgive them.'

Someone asked, 'Are you tired, Father?'

'No, I'm fine,' he mumbled, his eyes fixed on the floor. 'I only feel pain in the winter when it is cold. When spring comes, I am fine again. That is the way it always is.'

FOR THE BEST IN PAPERBACKS, LOOK FOR THE 🐧

In every corner of the world, on every subject under the sun, Penguin represents quality and variety – the very best in publishing today.

For complete information about books available from Penguin – including Puffins, Penguin Classics and Arkana – and how to order them, write to us at the appropriate address below. Please note that for copyright reasons the selection of books varies from country to country.

In the United Kingdom: Please write to *Dept E.P., Penguin Books Ltd, Harmondsworth, Middlesex, UB7 0DA.*

If you have any difficulty in obtaining a title, please send your order with the correct money, plus ten per cent for postage and packaging, to *PO Box No 11, West Drayton, Middlesex*

In the United States: Please write to *Dept BA, Penguin, 299 Murray Hill Parkway, East Rutherford, New Jersey 07073*

In Canada: Please write to *Penguin Books Canada Ltd, 2801 John Street, Markham, Ontario L3R 1B4*

In Australia: Please write to the *Marketing Department, Penguin Books Australia Ltd, P.O. Box 257, Ringwood, Victoria 3134*

In New Zealand: Please write to the *Marketing Department, Penguin Books (NZ) Ltd, Private Bag, Takapuna, Auckland 9*

In India: Please write to *Penguin Overseas Ltd, 706 Eros Apartments, 56 Nehru Place, New Delhi, 110019*

In the Netherlands: Please write to *Penguin Books Netherlands B.V., Postbus 195, NL–1380AD Weesp*

In West Germany: Please write to *Penguin Books Ltd, Friedrichstrasse 10–12, D–6000 Frankfurt/Main 1*

In Spain: Please write to *Longman Penguin España, Calle San Nicolas 15, E–28013 Madrid*

In Italy: Please write to *Penguin Italia s.r.l., Via Como 4, I-20096 Pioltello (Milano)*

In France: Please write to *Penguin Books Ltd, 39 Rue de Montmorency, F-75003 Paris*

In Japan: Please write to *Longman Penguin Japan Co Ltd, Yamaguchi Building, 2–12–9 Kanda Jimbocho, Chiyoda-Ku, Tokyo 101*

A SELECTION OF FICTION AND NON-FICTION

Perfume Patrick Süskind

It was after his first murder that Grenouille knew he was a genius. He was to become the greatest perfumer of all time, for he possessed the power to distil the very essence of love itself. 'Witty, stylish and ferociously absorbing' – *Observer*

A Confederacy of Dunces John Kennedy Toole

In this Pulitzer Prize-winning novel, in the bulky figure of Ignatius J. Reilly, an immortal comic character is born. 'I succumbed, stunned and seduced ... a masterwork of comedy' – *The New York Times*

In the Land of Oz Howard Jacobson

'The most successful attempt I know to grip the great dreaming Australian enigma by the throat and make it gargle' – *Evening Standard*. 'Sharp characterization, crunching dialogue and self-parody ... brilliantly funny' – *Literary Review*

Falconer John Cheever

Ezekiel Farragut, fratricide with a heroin habit, comes to Falconer Correctional Facility. His freedom is enclosed, his view curtailed by iron bars. But he is a man, none the less, and the vice, misery and degradation of prison change a man...

The Memory of War and Children in Exile: Poems 1968–83 James Fenton

'James Fenton is a poet I find myself again and again wanting to praise' – *Listener*. 'His assemblages bring with them tragedy, comedy, love of the world's variety, and the sadness of its moral blight' – *Observer*

The Bloody Chamber Angela Carter

In tales that glitter and haunt – strange nuggets from a writer whose wayward pen spills forth stylish, erotic, nightmarish jewels of prose – the old fairy stories live and breathe again, subtly altered, subtly changed.

A SELECTION OF FICTION AND NON-FICTION

Stories Satyajit Ray

'At once fantastic, realistically human, and occasionally frightening ... for sheer entertainment and pleasure Mr Ray's collection deserves the highest recommendation' – *The Times*

The Purple Decades Tom Wolfe

From Surfers to Moonies, from *The Electric Kool-Aid Acid Test* to *The Right Stuff*, a technicolour retrospective from the foremost chronicler of the gaudiest period in American history. 'Like Evelyn Waugh, Wolfe is a maestro of savage hilarity and a moralist beneath the skin' – *Newsweek*

Sugar and Other Stories A. S. Byatt

'Antonia Byatt's first collection of stories displays all her talents as a novelist, but spiced with an additional friskiness ... a bright sensual prose that seems to paint rather than describe' – Penelope Lively

The Moronic Inferno Martin Amis

'Really good reading and sharp, crackling writing. Amis has a beguiling mixture of confidence and courtesy, and most of his literary judgments – often twinned with interviews – seem sturdy, even when caustic, without being bitchy for the hell of it' – *Guardian*

Elizabeth Alone William Trevor

'With a fruitful marriage (and a quick, astonishing adulterous bounce) behind her, comfortable, amiable Mrs Aidallbery – Elizabeth – is in hospital for a hysterectomy ... A finely observed, gently sensitive comedy, delightful to read, like lived experience to remember' – *Daily Telegraph*

The Guide R. K. Narayan

Raju, recently released from prison, used to be India's most corrupt tourist guide. Then a peasant mistakes him for a holy man – and gradually he begins to play the part. 'The best of R. K. Narayan's enchanting novels' – *New Yorker*

A SELECTION OF FICTION AND NON-FICTION

The Book of Laughter and Forgetting Milan Kundera

'A whirling dance of a book ... a masterpiece full of angels, terror, ostriches and love ... No question about it. The most important novel published in Britain this year' – Salman Rushdie in the *Sunday Times*

Miami Joan Didion

'Joan Didion's Miami is at once an aggressively real city and a legendary domain to which Swift might well have posted Gulliver ... a work that combines intense imaginative vision with extraordinary argumentative force' – Jonathan Raban in the *Observer*

Milk and Honey Elizabeth Jolley

'In a claustrophobic family of Viennese refugees to Australia, the young boarder Jacob studies the cello, and is alternately pampered and terrified until his father dies and leaves him a fortune ... a quirky, brilliantly written study on the amorality of ignoring reality' – *The Times*

Einstein's Monsters Martin Amis

'This collection of five stories and an introductory essay ... announces an obsession with nuclear weapons; it also announces a new tonality in Amis's writing' – John Lanchester in the *London Review of Books*. 'He has never written to better effect' – John Carey in the *Sunday Times*

In the Heart of the Country J. M. Coetzee

In a web of reciprocal oppression in colonial South Africa, a white sheep-farmer makes a bid for salvation in the arms of a black concubine, while his embittered daughter dreams of and executes a bloody revenge. Or does she?

In Custody Anita Desai

Deven, a lecturer in a small town in northern India, is resigned to a life of mediocrity and empty dreams. Asked to interview Delhi's greatest poet, he discovers a new kind of dignity...

A SELECTION OF FICTION AND NON-FICTION

Cal Bernard Mac Laverty

Springing out of the fear and violence of Ulster, *Cal* is a haunting love story from a land where tenderness and innocence can only flicker briefly in the dark. 'Mac Laverty describes the sad, straitened, passionate lives of his characters with tremendously moving skill' – *Spectator*

The Rebel Angels Robertson Davies

A glittering extravaganza of wit, scatology, saturnalia, mysticism and erudite vaudeville. 'The kind of writer who makes you want to nag your friends until they read him so that they can share the pleasure' – *Observer*

Stars of the New Curfew Ben Okri

'Anarchical energy with authoritative poise ... an electrifying collection' – Graham Swift. 'Okri's work is obsessive and compelling, spangled with a sense of exotic magic and haunted by shadows ... reality re-dreamt with great conviction' – *Time Out*

The Magic Lantern Ingmar Bergman

'A kaleidoscope of memories intercut as in a film, sharply written and trimmed to the bone' – *Sunday Times*. 'The autobiography is exactly like the films: beautiful and repulsive; truthful and phoney; constantly startling' – *Sunday Telegraph*. 'Unique, reticent, revealing' – Lindsay Anderson

August in July Carlo Gébler

On the eve of the Royal Wedding, as the nation prepares for celebration, August Slemic's world falls apart. 'There is no question but that he must now be considered a novelist of major importance' – *Daily Telegraph*

The News from Ireland William Trevor

'An ability to enchant as much as chill has made Trevor unquestionably one of our greatest short-story writers' – *The Times*. 'A masterly collection' – *Daily Telegraph*

A CHOICE OF PENGUIN FICTION

The House of Stairs   Barbara Vine

'A masterly and hypnotic synthesis of past, present and terrifying future ... both compelling and disturbing' – *Sunday Times*. 'Not only ... a quietly smouldering suspense novel but also ... an accurately atmospheric portrayal of London in the heady '60s. Literally unputdownable' – *Time Out*

Other Women   Lisa Alther

From the bestselling author of *Kinflicks* comes this compelling novel of today's woman – and a heroine with whom millions of women will identify.

The Old Jest   Jennifer Johnston

Late summer near Dublin, 1920. Even before she meets the mysterious fugitive on the beach, eighteen-year-old Nancy has begun to sense that the old charmed life of the Anglo-Irish ascendancy simply cannot go on forever ... 'Subtle, moving and distinguished' – *Observer*

Your Lover Just Called   John Updike

Stories of Joan and Richard Maple – a couple multiplied by love and divided by lovers. Here is a portrait of a modern American marriage in all its mundane moments as only John Updike could draw it.

To Have and to Hold   Deborah Moggach

Attractive, radical and fecund, Viv has been lucky with life. In return, she is generous with her time and with her love: she can afford to be. And now Viv is giving her sister Ann – sterile, less glamorous, apparently conventional – the best present she can think of: a baby.

A CHOICE OF PENGUIN FICTION

The High Road   Edna O'Brien

Her long-awaited new novel of a lyrical love between two women. 'Contemporary and sophisticated ... *The High Road* is all that I wanted it to be ... the same emotional sensitivity, especially in the arena of sexual passion. The same authority of characterization' – *Guardian*

The Philosopher's Pupil   Iris Murdoch

'We are back, of course, with great delight, in the land of Iris Murdoch, which is like no other but Prospero's' – *Sunday Telegraph*. 'The most daring and original of all her novels' – A. N. Wilson

Paradise Postponed   John Mortimer

'Hats off to John Mortimer. He's done it again' – *Spectator*. Why does Simeon Simcox, the CND-marching Rector of Rapstone Fanner, leave his fortune not to his two sons but to an odious Tory Minister? A rumbustious, hilarious novel from the creator of Rumpole.

The Anatomy Lesson   Philip Roth

The famous forty-year-old writer Nathan Zuckerman decides to give it all up and become a doctor – and a pornographer – instead. 'The finest, boldest and funniest piece of fiction that Philip Roth has yet produced' – *Spectator*

Gabriel's Lament   Paul Bailey

'The best novel yet by one of the most careful fiction craftsmen of his generation' – *Guardian*. 'A magnificent novel, moving, eccentric and unforgettable. He has a rare feeling for language and an understanding of character which few can rival' – *Daily Telegraph*

A CHOICE OF PENGUIN FICTION

Sweet Desserts Lucy Ellmann

Winner of the Guardian Fiction Prize. 'A wild book ... interrupted by excerpts from cook books, authoritarian healthy-eating guides, pretentious theses on modern art, officious radio sex-advice shows, diaries, suicide notes...' – *Observer*. 'An enchanting, enchanted book' – Fay Weldon. 'Lucy Ellmann is an original' – *Guardian*

The Lost Language of Cranes David Leavitt

Owen Benjamin has a job, a wife, a son, a steady and well-ordered life, except for one small detail – Owen has spent nearly every Sunday of his married life in a gay porno movie theatre. 'An astonishingly mature and accomplished writer' – *Listener*

The Accidental Tourist Anne Tyler

How does a man addicted to routine – a man who flosses his teeth before love-making – cope with the chaos of everyday life? 'Now poignant, now funny ... Anne Tyler is brilliant' – *The New York Times Book Review*

Fiddle City Dan Kavanagh

'Scary insider's data on the airport sub-world, customs knowhow and smugglers' more sickening dodges are marvellously aerated by bubbles of Mr Kavanagh's very dry, sly, wide-ranging and Eighties humour' – *Sunday Times*

The Rachel Papers Martin Amis

A stylish, sexy and ribaldly funny novel by the author of *Money*. 'Remarkable' – *Listener*. 'Very funny indeed' – *Spectator*

BY THE SAME AUTHOR

Silence

'*Silence* is a profound and moving book ... It is first and foremost the story of one man's journey towards self-knowledge. And that is the only significant subject-matter with which any serious novelist has to do' – *The Times*

'Mr Endo is giving deep thought to the most basic problems of truth and how in exchanging it among ourselves we misconstruct its nature at every step – *Spectator*

'One of the finest novels of our time' – Graham Greene

'A crucial book: both a great story and a re-examination of the Christian myth' – *Sunday Telegraph*

The Samurai

'Powerful ... beautifully written ... a fascinating narrative with its double perspective from East to West' – *New Statesman*

'Endo is really like no one else ... as that rarity, a Japanese Catholic, he has found a border territory – of cultural and psychological clash – which is all his own' – *Observer*

Scandal

'Evil and guilt are the shadowy devils in this Dostoyevskean tale of hidden dreams. *Scandal* is a subtle, eerie and fascinating book by a writer of rare perception and disquieting honesty' – *Evening Standard*

'A spiritual thriller, told with a classical precision and extraordinary tension ... Endo is one of the very few great novelists at work today' – *Listener*